Sacked when his first division team is relegated, football manager Mac Murphy realizes that any job is better than none, so he gratefully takes on ailing Dunmore United.

The club can hardly be said to have a lot going for it. Fighting for survival at the bottom of the fourth division, with a neglected ground and poor facilities, there's also the problem of vandalism as local kids have nowhere to go and nothing to do. The club owner, Rasputin Jones, is a devious character who's only interested in making money. His method of solving vandalism is to ban the kids from the ground. But Mac's methods prove more effective: he invites them to start a Junior Supporters' Club and it becomes a very successful outlet for their energies.

As Mac continues to battle with opinionated members of the board who've had their own way for too long, so the Junior Supporters have to cope with their difficulties too. Has Boxer been framed or did he really steal the money from their fund-raising disco?

With problems on and off the pitch, Dunmore United seems to be hitting rock bottom. But then Rasputin buys a new player, a former international, who he's convinced will save the club ...

This exciting and fast-paced story, based on the popular television series, will be enjoyed by football lovers and loathers alike!

MURPHY'S MOB

by Michael Saunders
based on the television series by Brian Finch

PUFFIN BOOKS

Puffin Books, Penguin Books Ltd, Harmondsworth, Middlesex, England
Penguin Books, 625 Madison Avenue, New York, New York 10022, U.S.A.
Penguin Books Australia Ltd, Ringwood, Victoria, Australia
Penguin Books Canada Ltd, 2801 John Street, Markham, Ontario, Canada L3R 1B4
Penguin Books (N.Z.) Ltd, 182–190 Wairau Road, Auckland 10, New Zealand

First published 1982

Filmset by Northumberland Press Ltd, Gateshead, Tyne and Wear
Made and printed in Great Britain by
Richard Clay (The Chaucer Press) Ltd, Bungay, Suffolk
Set in VIP Plantin

1

Dunmore United was a lousy football club. They were bottom of the fourth division, and they had almost lost their place in that last season, but when Mac Murphy saw they were looking for a new manager he was in no position to be choosy. He'd been demoted himself; sacked by the first division club he'd been managing when they were relegated last season. His wife, Elaine, was all in favour when he mentioned Dunmore United. And so the two of them drove down to the Midlands one drizzly summer's afternoon to keep an appointment with Dunmore's new owner, Rasputin Jones.

The club was every bit as run down as Mac had expected. It was all locked up, there was no one around, the sign was hanging off the gate, and as Mac and his wife picked their way through the passageway beneath the terraces in their fruitless search for Jones, they tripped over some empty beer cans which had been left lying around.

'Well,' said Mac, surveying the pitch and neglected terraces.

'You don't have to take the job, Mac.'

'Course I don't. There's always the dole.'

'It wouldn't bother me if you got out of football management altogether.'

'I know.' Mac grinned at her suddenly. He knew she meant it.

There came a shout from behind them. 'Hoy!' They turned and saw an elderly groundsman hurrying towards them. 'What are you two up to?' he said, grumpy and aggressive. He spoke as if they might be going to dig up his turf.

'I'm looking for Mr Jones. Mr Rasputin Jones,' said Mac.

'Then you're unlucky.'

'You're the groundsman?' Mac asked him.

The old man nodded. He wasn't giving anything more away. 'I know who you are,' he said, grimly. 'Saw you on the telly. Day you got sacked.'

That was the sort of remark which needled Elaine. She hated anyone to get at Mac. 'Have you any idea where we might find Mr Jones?' she asked the old man sharply.

'I might,' said the old man.

'Well, is it a secret?' Elaine was irritated. 'Or could you give us a clue?'

'Depends.'

'On what?'

'On whether he's off golfing.'

'And if he isn't off golfing,' said Mac. He rather liked this old codger.

Perhaps the old man sensed it, for he decided to give something away at last.

'The rink,' he said, with a sour toss of his head. 'Roller rink next door. Making a fortune out of it, he is.' He gave a scornful sniff. 'Den of iniquity if you ask me.'

They did not find Rasputin Jones at the roller rink, or not at first, but it was there that Mac had his first encounter with the United fans. He and Elaine stood outside the locked door marked 'Manager' and surveyed the scene: noisy music and loads of local kids whizzing around on hissing skates beneath blue, green and pink strobe lights. Elaine was grumbling quietly about Rasputin's absence – he had agreed to meet them at three – when a fight broke out. To the regulars, it was an everyday occurrence. Boxer Reed and Gerry Jackson were leaders of rival gangs from the same estate. Today it was Boxer who skimmed up behind Gerry, skating with his girlfriend Sheila, and sent him flying. Gerry gave chase, and brought Boxer down with a rugger tackle; the two boys went crashing through a crowd of younger skaters. A small girl started to cry.

'Crikey, isn't there any supervision in this place?' said Mac, and never one to stand on the side-lines, he waded into the fray, crossing the rink and yanking the two boys apart.

'All right, knock it off,' he said. 'What's all this about?'

'He started it,' said Gerry. He was a good-looking, sturdy boy.

'He got me last week,' protested Boxer, who was big and tough-looking.

'I said that's *enough*,' said Mac.

'What the hell's going on here?' said a voice behind him. Mac turned, and saw a small, wiry man with a neat haircut and suede trousers. It was Rasputin. He swore when he saw which boys were in trouble again. He slung the two of them out and told them not to come back, and then, without bothering with introductions – or apologies, for meeting Mac in the wrong place at the wrong time – he whisked him and Elaine into his office, where he gave them coffee and told them all about himself.

Rasputin was an ambitious, aggressive little man, who couldn't have been more than thirty. He'd been a pop singer, star of Rasputin and the Freaks. He showed the Murphys a picture of himself at the height of his fame, his hair streaked all the colours of the rainbow. He laughed at it, but proudly, Elaine thought. He was pleased with himself for the money he'd made – and, judging by the office they now sat in, there had been quite a lot of it – and for having the sense to get out of the music business while he was still winning. He told them that he'd been bored and rich, that the fans had been bored and broke, and that he'd bought the club, sacked the manager, and paid off the overdraft.

'Just like that,' said Elaine. Mac could tell that she thought this young tycoon opposite them was a bit too big for his boots.

'It's the way I do business, Mrs Murphy,' said Rasputin. 'If you're a winner for me – I'm a generous man. If you aren't ...' He shrugged. 'Sorry.' He turned to Mac. 'So, Big Mac,' he said. 'Are you in or out?'

'I'm here,' said Mac, cautiously.

'Seen the ground?'

'We had a quick look. I'd like to see over it properly.'

'Right,' said Rasputin, swallowing the remains of his coffee, and getting up as if Mac's words had shot him from his seat. 'I'll show you. It's hardly the Dell. But then you aren't Laurie McMenemy either.'

Mac registered the truth of that with a small nod. Elaine gave Rasputin a poisonous look.

Unbeknown to Mac and Rasputin, they were not the only ones who had moved from the rink to the ground that afternoon. Thrown out of the rink, Gerry and Boxer saw no reason not to continue their hostilities over at the club. At first each little group crept through the passageways beneath the stand and around the club, keeping a wary eye out for each other and for Sam Fletcher, the groundsman. Then Wurzel found some buckets, which gave Boxer an idea. They filled them with water, and climbed up on the terraces, leaning over the bannister to see if Gerry, who had Gonk, a black kid, and a little swot called the Prof in tow, was anywhere in sight. They had to wait a bit, but finally they came, and as they passed beneath Boxer and Wurzel they were doused with cold water. With triumphant yells, Boxer and Wurzel scrambled down over the side of the terrace and landed on their soaking enemies. In the fight that ensued, they sent each other crashing into crates of empties which were stacked along the passageway. By the time they had finished, there was broken glass littered everywhere.

Mac was with Rasputin in the small dingy room which was to be his office, gazing at a dog-eared photograph of Dunmore United in its better days, when the sound of the fracas reached them. Rasputin shot out of the door in seconds and raced towards the noise, but at the sound of his yelling the boys vanished.

'Who are these kids?' Mac asked him, as he caught up with him to see scattered crates and bits of brown, broken glass everywhere.

'Locals,' said Rasputin, angrily. 'From the estate. The same ones who give me such a hard time around the rink.'

'Can't you speak to their headmasters?'

'They're on holiday,' said Rasputin. 'Anyway, this lot don't even listen to their own fathers. And the police are useless, too. I've asked them to put a watch on the ground but –' He shook his head. 'But I know someone who can sort it out,' he said grimly.

'Who?'

'Me. Who else?'

'What are you going to do?'

'You'll see,' said Rasputin. 'Or will you?' He remembered suddenly that he was interviewing Mac for the job. 'Are you in or out?'

Mac raised a craggy eyebrow at his wife who was standing a few feet away, surveying the damage.

'Your decision, love,' she said.

'We'll give it a go,' said Mac.

'Good,' said Rasputin, kicking a crate aside, and moving swiftly towards the forecourt of the club.

'Hey,' Mac called after him. 'When do I start?'

'What's wrong with now?' said Rasputin, and departed leaving Mac and Elaine where they stood, to think through the practicalities of moving house and where they would stay in the meantime, and whether they were doing the right thing in the first place.

Mac was to learn that Rasputin always liked everything done by yesterday. Next morning when he turned up at the club, he could hear loud, frantic barking. Rounding a corner, he saw old Sam shaking his spade at two fierce, rather mangy alsatian dogs who were tethered to a none-too-solid-looking drainpipe.

'Dunno what you want them for,' he told Mac, dourly. 'Dogs. Never could stand 'em.'

Mac said nothing at the time, but when Rasputin came cannoning in to see him an hour or so later he had something to say.

'Whose are those dogs, then?'

'Mine,' said Rasputin. 'I bought 'em this morning. Bargain offer. From a security firm that's just gone bust.'

'You're not seriously thinking of letting those brutes run round loose?' Mac asked. Beside Rasputin he seemed very calm and solid, almost ponderous.

'Only when we've gone home,' said Rasputin.

'You're joking. You have to be.'

'What's the matter? Don't you like dogs?'

'Yes. I like dogs,' said Mac. 'I just don't like the idea of dogs chewing up kids. Just because they happen to be doing a bit of trespassing.'

'A bit of trespassing?' said Rasputin. 'They're wrecking the place.'

'I'm sorry, Dad,' said Mac, firmly. 'But dogs are out.'

'Come again.'

'You heard. I'm not having dogs like that running round my football club without adequate supervision.'

'*Whose* football club?' said Rasputin.

'*My* football club,' said Mac, holding his ground. 'So long as I'm managing it, I do it my way. No dogs.'

'And if I don't happen to agree with you?'

'You can tear up my contract.'

Rasputin stared at Mac angrily. He wasn't used to his employees refusing to do things his way, but he could see that the older man wasn't going to budge.

'All right,' he said, finally. 'You're the manager. For the moment, anyway. Just how good a manager we'll see when the season starts. In the meantime, you've got a problem. Someone's kicking *your* football ground to bits. The one *I* happen to own. And if you don't do something about it, I will. Whether it costs me your services or not.'

'I'll do something about it,' said Mac. Quite what, he had no idea.

Boxer and Gerry, of course, knew nothing about the dogs, but they were shaping up for another round in their endless running battle. That evening, when Boxer and his sister Jean were washing up the tea things, Gerry's lieutenant, Gonk, came to the door.

'Geronimo wants to see you,' he told Boxer, who was keeping the door of the flat half-closed so that Jean wouldn't hear. 'Says he wants to sort it out with you. Once and for all. Just the two of you on your own, down at The Place.'

'Tell him I'll be there,' said Boxer. He wasn't afraid of Gerry. He could look after himself; after all, he boxed for his school.

'I didn't know Gonk was a mate of yours,' said Jean suspiciously, when Boxer came back into the kitchen.

'He's not.'

'He knocks around with Gerry Jackson, doesn't he?'

'Yeah.'

Jean eyed her brother shrewdly. She'd heard the police had been on the estate earlier that day, trying to find out who had been responsible for the trouble at the ground the day before.

'What's going on, Boxer?' she asked him.

'Nothing to do with you,' said Boxer. He grabbed his anorak and made for the door.

'If Dad finds out, he'll kill you.'

The Place was the ground. They never missed a match there, any of them, though they all complained the club was just a load of rubbish. When Gerry arrived there was a panda car parked at the gate and he ducked round a corner, waiting impatiently for a young and conscientious police constable to try all the gates. No sooner had he driven off than Gerry was scrambling up on the wall. He was anxious to get into position before Boxer arrived. Only as he jumped down on the other side did he see the dogs. They were barking and lunging towards him. He drew back terrified and then realized, with relief, that they were tied up.

'Shush,' he told them, as he eased past. They barked louder than ever. Fortunately there was no one to hear them – or, at least, so Gerry thought. He slipped through the shadowy passages and out on to the pitch to wait in goal in the fading evening light for Boxer to arrive.

He saw something white moving in the dark shadows at the other end of the pitch and realized it was the stripes on Boxer's anorak. He must have come in from the other side. He saw him vault the rails and come to stand in the opposing goal. Gerry moved forward. He was scared now. He didn't relish the fight ahead. Boxer had started to move up the pitch, too. Gerry didn't take his eyes off him for a second. In fact he was so intent on watching his old enemy that he didn't notice Mac Murphy at all. Mac, who had been working late in his office, trying to get to grips with his new job, had been drawn outside by the barking. Now, as he watched the two lads stalking towards each other up the empty pitch, he had a brainwave.

They had reached the centre circle by the time he returned to the pitch with the two dogs, on leads, by his side. The boys began to circle each other, warily. Then, as Boxer put up his fists and Gerry moved in as if to close with him, Mac gave a yell.

'Hold it right there,' he shouted. His voice sounded loud and stentorian in the empty stadium. Then, as the two boys made as if to run for it, he shouted again. 'I wouldn't – not unless you fancy your chances of out-running these dogs. You come over here. Slowly.'

And so they did, and Mac took them upstairs to his dingy office, only tying up the dogs when they were safely trapped in his corridor. He sat down and inter-rogated them. He wanted to know who they were and what it was about. Neither of them could tell him, for neither of them knew. They had just been enemies so long that it had become a habit.

'He's a bighead,' said Boxer lamely, in the end.

'Oh, and I suppose you're a shrinking violet,' said Mac, sarcastically. His eye fell on the small metal badge on Boxer's anorak. 'What's the badge?' he said.

'United,' said Boxer, sullenly.

'Oh, I see. Fan, then?'

'Yeah.'

'You too?'

'Course,' said Gerry, with some pride.

'No, you're not,' said Mac, contemptuously.

'We come every week,' said Gerry.

'That still doesn't make you a fan,' said Mac. 'I'll tell you about fans, son. Real fans. They aren't the people who just come every week. Looking for aggro with the other so-called fans. Causing trouble on the terraces and getting the club and the game a bad name. 'Cos I bet that's just what you do, isn't it?'

The boys said nothing. Then Gerry, looking up and catching Mac's eye, muttered, 'Sometimes.'

'Right,' said Mac. 'And fans like you we can do without. 'Cos, like I said, you aren't real fans. Real fans care about the club, even a fleabitten place like this one. So don't tell me you're a fan, son, 'cos if you were you wouldn't be here every night doing damage to the place you should be doing your best to build up.'

'How could we do that?' asked Boxer, genuinely curious.

'Well, for starters, join the Supporters' Club,' said Mac.

'He won't let us.'

'Who won't?'

'Cassidy.'

'Who's Cassidy?'

'The bloke who runs the Supporters' Club,' said Gerry.

'Oh yeah,' said Mac. He'd met Cassidy earlier that day and hadn't cared much for him – a pale, thin-lipped punctilious, little man. Still, he wasn't going to run him down on first impressions, particularly not to these two little tearaways. 'Why won't he let you join?' he asked them.

'He reckons we're just scruff. Troublemakers.'

'Well, aren't you? Sometimes?'

'Suppose so,' muttered Boxer.

'So behave yourselves. And perhaps one day he'll change his mind about you.'

And then he proceeded to tell them about himself: how he had spent half his life scrapping with this other kid, whom he thought was a bighead, until one day they'd called a truce and decided to try getting on with each other. 'And do you know what?' he told the boys. 'Not only was it a lot less painful after that, but he became my best mate. And still is. You want to try it sometime.'

There was a pause when he'd finished, and Gerry shot Boxer a sideways look, but Boxer wasn't letting on.

'Go on, scram, the pair of you,' said Mac. 'And whatever you do, don't let me catch you messing about on the ground again. Otherwise I really will set the dogs on you.'

The next day Boxer stayed indoors. Wurzel came round to see where he was, and he was there when Gerry knocked on the door.

'What do you want?' said Boxer. They didn't normally carry their fights into the enemy camp like this.

'To talk to you,' Gerry said. Then, seeing Wurzel: 'On our own.'

Boxer hesitated for a second and then indicated with a nod that Wurzel should leave.

'I'll be right outside, Boxer, right?' said Wurzel. He was a shambling, scruffy kid, always in tatty jeans. Now as he left the room he gave Gerry a mean look.

Gerry, safe now that there were no witnesses – he knew Wurzel would just have thought him chicken – put it to Boxer that maybe Mac had a point. Boxer shrugged, as Gerry had known he would. He was never one for climbing down. Gerry pressed on with the second part of his idea: that they should ask Mac to give them premises at the ground where they could start a Junior Supporters' Club. For the first time Boxer showed a flicker of interest.

'He'll never do it.'

'We don't know till we ask,' said Gerry.

The room Mac gave them was little more than a filthy store cupboard, crammed with old equipment and some broken chairs, but the kids set to work with a will, both gangs, and cleared it out. By the following week they had managed to scrounge an old table tennis table and a darts board, and in a grubby sort of way the club was beginning to look quite homely.

There were to be a few problems before the club got started, however. First of all there was Derek Cassidy. When he saw the sign on the door – DUNMORE UNITED – JUNIOR SUPPORTERS' CLUB – he came barging in and demanded to know what was going on. Why had nobody told him about it, he wanted to know.

'We thought you were a bit old for it, Mr Cassidy,' said Boxer, mischievously, and everyone giggled. That did it. Cassidy pursed his thin lips and narrowed his eyes, and went off to find Mac Murphy.

'This Junior Supporters' Club nonsense,' he began. Mac raised a bushy eyebrow at the pale figure with the clipboard under his arm. Cassidy often carried a clipboard. He was at his happiest in committee meetings when he could refer to agendas and halt the debate with points of order.

'Nonsense?' said Mac.

'We already have a Supporters' Club here at United. And a thriving one at that. Thanks to all the work me and the lads have put in over the years.'

'Which doesn't cater for youngsters, I understand,' said Mac.

'The right sort of youngster, it does,' said Cassidy, self-righteously.

'Oh yes?' said Mac. 'And what sort of youngsters would those be?'

'Decent, respectable kids,' said Cassidy. 'Like my own lad. Certainly not the likes of those scruffs from that tatty housing estate opposite.'

That clinched it. Mac had disliked this man instinctively, on first sight. Now he knew he was right. He put his elbows on his desk and leaned his large, craggy head on his hands.

'I'll tell you something about that tatty housing estate,

Mr Cassidy,' he said. 'It reminds me of somewhere, you know.'

'Oh, yes?' said Cassidy politely.

'The tatty housing estate I was brought up on. Back in Scotland.'

There was an awkward pause. Cassidy's pale face turned bright pink.

'Look, I'm not a snob, of course,' he said.

'Of course,' said Mac, ironic.

'But those kids are troublemakers,' insisted Cassidy. 'They've terrorized the place for years.'

'I know,' said Mac. 'That's why I told them to go ahead and form their own Supporters' Club. And ever since we haven't had a spot of trouble. Nothing.'

'But they can't run a club,' said Cassidy.

'How do we know?' said Mac. 'Until we let them have a try?' And he would not be budged. Cassidy became angry.

'Look, if it was up to me they wouldn't even be allowed at matches,' he said.

'But then it isn't up to you, is it, Mr Cassidy?' said Mac. 'And it's my opinion that at present this club needs all the help it can get. Even from that tatty housing estate. Because beggars can't be choosers.'

Cassidy left Mac's office furious and humiliated. He thought for a while, and then decided to find out what Rasputin had to say about it.

'The kids from the estate?' said Rasputin, disbelievingly. 'The little terrorists who've been giving us such a hard time?'

'You didn't know about it then, Mr Jones,' said Cassidy, feigning surprise but inwardly gleeful. 'Well. I am glad I told you. I wasn't going to bother you, I mean, I know what a busy man you are. It's just that it does cut across something we're doing ourselves, actually. The Supporters' Club does have plans in hand to found its own junior section. It's actually on the agenda for our next committee meeting.' This was quite untrue. The idea had come to Cassidy as he waited to be shown into Rasputin's office. 'If *only* Mr Murphy had mentioned it to me. Or you, for that matter,' said Cassidy, regretfully.

'All right, Derek, leave it with me,' said Rasputin abruptly. He didn't much care for the chairman of the Supporters' Club either.

'Right, Mr Jones. Sorry to have bothered you,' said Cassidy, obsequiously. He let himself out of the office, delighted at the trouble ahead for Mac.

On his way to ask Mac what the hell he thought he was playing at, Rasputin was dumbfounded to see one of his two fierce guard dogs playing with the black kid called Gonk.

'Hoy! You!' he shouted, and as Gonk turned to see who it was he wanted: 'Yes. You. Come here.'

Gonk picked up the dog's lead, which was trailing, and led him over towards Rasputin.

'What do you think you're doing with that dog?' he said, exasperated. 'I bought those dogs to keep you out of here —'

'I'm taking him for a walk,' said Gonk. 'A big dog needs exercise.'

'Give him here,' said Rasputin.

Gonk moved forward to hand over the lead, but the dog knew whom he preferred between Gonk and Rasputin. As Rasputin stretched out his hand to take the lead, he started to growl menacingly. Rasputin took a step backwards.

'Get that thing away from me,' he said nervously.

'Thought you said you wanted him,' said Gonk.

'Just hang on to him, all right?' said Rasputin. The incident made him tetchier than ever.

'Just what the hell goes on here?' he demanded, as he charged through the door of Mac's office. 'What the hell's all this about a Junior Supporters' Club?'

'You've been talking to Derek Cassidy,' said Mac.

'And if I have? He's a good bloke. He does a lot of good work for this club, does Derek Cassidy!'

'So he tells me,' said Mac, wryly.

'You were saying? About this Junior Supporters' Club bit?'

'No great mystery about it,' said Mac. 'A good old British principle in fact. If you can't lick 'em, get 'em to join you. You asked me to stop the vandalism, right?'

'Right.'

'I've stopped it.'

Having put himself on the line for the children, Mac was concerned they should make a go of the club. He looked in that afternoon and, though it was peaceful enough, they didn't seem to have done very much towards actually organizing themselves into a club.

'Who's going to run this club?' he asked them.

'We all are,' they chorused.

'Don't talk daft,' said Mac. 'You can't run a club along those lines, man. That's mob rule, that is. You need organization. A chairman. A secretary, treasurer, committee.'

'All right,' said Sheila, Gerry's girlfriend. 'We'll have an election.'

It was then that the trouble started. Boxer's crowd nominated him for chairman, and Gerry's lot proposed him. It looked as if the two gangs were lining up to split the new club right down the middle.

Sheila, and Boxer's sister, Jean, could see what was coming; and they saw too that the way out of the dilemma was to propose an outsider. Jean suggested that Sheila should stand.

'They'd never vote for a girl,' said Sheila.

'Well, we'll have to get a few girls along then, won't we?' said Jean. 'To vote for you.'

And so they did. Mac, who had agreed to chair the election meeting for them, was as surprised as anyone to see a dozen girls sitting among the boys. And he was even more taken aback when one of them, a petite, rather pretty girl called Jennifer Lee, pulled him up for using the word 'chairman'.

'There's no such thing as a "chairman",' she told him firmly.

'There isn't?' said Mac.

'No, sir. Not these days. It's "chairperson".'

Mac gave her a look. He didn't hold with all this women's lib nonsense. But Jennifer was smiling at him sweetly, and so he decided to play along.

'We're here to elect ourselves a chairperson, right?'

'Thank you,' said Jennifer. And promptly proposed Sheila, to an outcry from the boys.

Mac saw immediately what the girls were up to and backed them up. And so a vote was taken, and although there were fewer girls than boys there the boys' vote was split between their two leaders, and Sheila easily beat the pair of them.

'That was a rotten trick,' said Gerry, furious with her. He hadn't expected his girlfriend to stand against him.

'I did it for the club's sake,' said Sheila. 'You know what would have happened if I hadn't. And, anyway, I still need a secretary and a treasurer.'

Although the club's immediate collapse had been averted, it was not to be expected that two groups who had loathed one another for so long could become one club without a few squabbles along the way.

They'd decided that in order to attract new members they would have to redecorate the clubroom; and the first step towards that was to strip all the old, stained wallpaper from the walls. It was while they were doing this that a fight broke out that was nearly the end of them.

Neither Gerry nor Boxer was there at the time. The others were soaking the wallpaper and scraping it off, when Wurzel, who was a messy kid at the best of times, set a full bucket of water down clumsily beside the Prof. A great dollop of water slopped over the Prof's shoes.

'Watch it!' said the Prof. He was a small, scholarly, rather fastidious child, who, although he lived on the estate and was part of Gerry's crowd, attended a private school. He spoke differently from the rest of them, and Wurzel started taking the mick.

'Oh, sorry old boy. Humble apologies and all that.'

'Funny!' said the Prof. Wurzel grinned down on him condescendingly and patted his head.

'Leave him alone!' called Gonk.

'You what?' said Wurzel.

'You heard. Leave him alone.'

He turned back to his scraping. As he did so, Wurzel flicked water at his back. Gonk froze for a second, then turned and grabbed the bucket. Wurzel, seeing what was in store for him, tried to wrestle it from him, with the result that most of the water ended up all over Gonk.

'Right,' said Gonk, livid. He picked up another bucket and let Wurzel have its entire scummy contents. Within seconds everyone was joining in and there was water flying all over the place.

'Stop it! Stop it!' shouted Jean desperately, but nobody listened.

It was unfortunate that Rasputin Jones should have chosen that very moment to walk in. He caught a great whoosh of water and soggy scraps of old wallpaper full in the face. A horrified silence fell on the children.

'We're awfully sorry,' said Jean helplessly, as Rasputin removed a wet strip of paper from his hair.

'I should think you are,' said Rasputin, looking down

at his ruined suit. 'A hundred and fifty guineas this cost. You just lost yourselves a clubhouse.'

Mac was furious with them too. As far as he was concerned, they'd behaved like the yobboes that people had always said they were. In vain the children begged him to give them a second chance. In the end it was Elaine who managed to persuade him, by pointing out that, with no Junior Supporters' Club to distract them, the kids might turn all their energies to destroying the club again.

'I've told you, love,' he said, exasperated. 'It's Rasputin's decision. There's nothing I can do.'

He thought about it all the same, and by the next morning he'd come up with an idea. There had been a reporter, Terry Banks, from the local radio station, after him for an interview all week. Mac got on to him.

'I can give you an interview today, if you like,' he said. 'But on one condition. I want you to pretend that we recorded it last week.'

'Suits me,' said the young reporter, puzzled.

Rasputin was driving along in his white Rolls-Royce, on his way to play golf, when he heard Mac's voice coming over the car radio. At first it was all good stuff about his plans for the team, and Rasputin listened appreciatively. He'd done the right thing, employing Murphy. Then: 'And what's all this about a Junior Supporters' Club?' asked the reporter. Rasputin stiffened. 'Well, you see, these kids are the fans of tomorrow' – Rasputin slammed on the brakes – 'and if we could give them their own clubhouse, encourage them to build it up' – Rasputin reversed the car roughly into a side road – 'instead of trying to knock it down' – Rasputin put his foot on the accelerator and sped back in the direction of the club – 'well, it might solve the problem, right?'

*

Mac heard Rasputin coming along the corridor to his office. He hastily switched off his little trannie and stuffed it in a drawer as Rasputin burst in.

'What's the idea?' demanded Rasputin.

'How do you mean?'

'You know what I'm on about. The piece you just did on Radio Fairborough.'

'Oh yes, that,' said Mac easily. 'Yes, we recorded that last week. Has it gone out, then?'

'You didn't hear it?'

Mac shook his head. 'Why? It was all right, wasn't it? Just the usual chat.' Then he put his hand over his mouth in feigned consternation. 'Wait a minute, though – oh no – he didn't go and use that stuff I gave him about the Junior Supporters' Club, did he?'

'That's right,' said Rasputin, grimly.

Mac hit the side of his head in mock frustration. 'I meant to ring him. Tell him to cut it all out. I mean, what's it going to look like? After me coming out with all that stuff about what a good thing it was. When the next thing they hear is that you've slung them out on their ear. And why. The papers will eat us alive, won't they?'

Rasputin folded his arms, and looked at Mac, coldly.

'You don't think if we were to give them another chance – just one –' Mac hesitated. 'What do you think?'

'I'll tell you what I think, mate,' said Rasputin. He knew he had no option now but to allow the kids back in. 'I think from now on I'm going to have to watch you. Very closely.'

3

They were back in the clubhouse, but they knew what a close shave it had been, and they knew they would have to do something to make the Junior Supporters' Club work this time. The problem was money. Nobody was going to want to be a member of what they all agreed was a dump. And without members – or rather their subscriptions – they couldn't afford to decorate the place to make it more attractive. They'd worked out that everything they needed in the way of materials came to almost forty pounds.

'We could ask Mac,' suggested Sheila.

Boxer was dubious. 'You know what he said. We had to stand on our own feet.'

'He can only say no,' said Jean.

'Yeah, I know,' said Boxer. 'And will.'

They decided to ask him anyway, but it was not so easy getting hold of him these days. The club's first league match was only two weeks away, and Mac was busy training his players hard. He didn't like the kids interrupting his training sessions. This particular morning he had a visitor as well, a fleshy man in a camel coat, whom Boxer recognized as Charlie Russell.

'Used to be chairman,' he told the others.

'Of what?' asked Sheila, ignorant.

'Of Dunmore United, stupid,' said Boxer. 'I hope that toe-rag of a son isn't with him.'

25

He was. At that moment, as the others watched Mac crossing from the gym to his office with Charlie Russell, Bernie, his son, and his mate Scobie had wandered into the Junior Supporters' clubroom. Gonk was alone in there, grooming Rover, one of Rasputin's guard dogs which Mac had decided to keep. Dog and boy looked up when the two kids came in.

'Yeah?' said Gonk.

'Just looking round,' said Bernie. 'Any objections?' He was a cocky little kid, a flashy dresser.

'Suppose not,' said Gonk.

'That your dog?' said Scobie. He was smaller than Bernie, and by and large he did what Bernie told him.

'It's the club mascot,' said Gonk, drawing the brush the length of the dog's back and then pulling a thick wad of hairs from the bristles.

'That old flea-bag?' said Scobie. 'The club mascot?' He stuck out a toe to poke the dog, who was rather thin and mangy. The dog gave a low growl.

'You'd better watch it,' said Gonk. 'He knows every word you say, you know.'

'This it, then?' said Bernie, sauntering to the other side of the room. 'This Junior Supporters' Club they were on about last week?'

'Yeah.'

'What a tip,' said Bernie.

'Won't be when we've decorated it.'

'Can anybody join?'

'Yeah,' said Gonk, torn between a desire for new members and his dislike for this cocky little kid. 'Cost you, mind.'

'How much?'

'A quid for starters. Then 20p a week subs.'

'Peanuts,' said Bernie. He was just digging in his back pocket for the money when Boxer and the others came back. Boxer stopped short when he saw Bernie.

'What do you want, Russell?' he said.

Bernie grinned. 'We want to join your club. Don't we, Scobie?'

Scobie nodded.

'No chance,' said Boxer.

'If we want to join, you can't stop us,' said Bernie.

'Want to bet?' said Boxer.

'Look – his dad's on the board you know –' said Scobie, in an insinuating whine.

'I couldn't care less if his grandad was Ron Greenwood. Now go on. On your bikes both of you.'

He moved towards Bernie, who put up his fists threateningly, and then, realizing he was no match for Boxer, put them down again.

'Come on, Scobie,' he said.

'What was all that about?' asked Gerry, amazed, as the door shut after them.

'Yeah,' said Sheila. 'I thought we were trying to attract new members.'

'Not members like Bernie Russell and Scobie Beeson,' said Boxer grimly. He knew Bernie of old, from the days when he used to play soccer for a club over at Broadshore. He knew what a troublemaker he was, and how his dad, who was a successful bookie, spoiled him rotten. He told the others about the time Bernie had offered to get his dad to buy the whole team a new strip. 'We told him not to bother. Because there was just one condition. Bernie wanted guaranteed places on the team for him and Scobie every week. Even though they were rubbish players.'

'Cheeky devils,' said Sheila.

'And that wasn't all,' said Boxer. 'Stuff kept on getting nicked. It got so you couldn't leave anything lying around the changing rooms. We could never prove it was Bernie, but when we kicked them out, the nicking stopped. Just like that.'

'But if he could have anything he wanted, why did he go nicking?' asked Gonk.

''Cos he can't help himself, can he,' said Boxer. ''Cos he's bent. Just like they reckon his old fellow is.'

Mac hadn't met Bernie's old fellow before that morning, and he didn't like him any more than Gonk had liked Bernie. He couldn't make out why Charlie Russell had come to see him in the first place.

'Just dropped in to wish you luck,' he told Mac. 'You'll need it.'

'Don't we all?' said Mac.

'Quite so, squire, quite so,' said Charlie, and then proceeded to tell Mac that he'd been a mite surprised when Rasputin had suggested bringing him in. 'I mean, let's be honest, you didn't have the best of seasons last time out. With your previous club.'

Mac gazed at the bulky, affluent, smiling man opposite him. 'Well, I suppose that's true, Mr Russell,' he said, levelly. 'But then come to think of it – you weren't having much of one yourself, were you? Till Mr Jones took over.'

Charlie Russell's grin slipped a little at that. 'Yes, well, there were good reasons for that,' he said.

'In my experience there always are in football. When things are going wrong.'

'Just so,' said Charlie. 'No, don't get me wrong. Every confidence, really.'

'Why, thank you, Mr Russell,' said Mac, wryly.

'So. Onward and upward. See you in gaol.'

'Right,' said Mac. He watched the former chairman leave his office, and hoped he wouldn't see too much of him in the future.

When Charlie Russell heard that his son – *his* son – had been denied membership of the Junior Supporters'

Club, he was back at the ground looking for Mac in no time at all. Unfortunately Mac had gone home, his first early night since he had started at United, and it was Derek Cassidy whom Russell met. Cassidy lost no time in informing Russell that the Junior Supporters' Club was nothing to do with him, that it was just a gang of scruffy kids.

'So they've turned young Bernie away, have they?' he said. 'Dear, dear. Well, I wish I could say I was surprised but in all honesty I can't. I tell you, Mr Russell, I sometimes wonder who is running this club these days, Mac Murphy or those kids. They're a law unto themselves. And cheek. I've never heard anything like it in my life. But say so much as a word to Mac and he takes their side every time. I'd say you'd be wasting your time tackling Mac about them – but Mr Jones now. I happen to know he has a very different opinion of them.'

Rasputin, as Cassidy had predicted, was very annoyed. He came storming into the kids' clubroom the next day to tell them exactly what he thought of them.

'You get something very clear in your heads,' he told them. 'If this is going to be the Dunmore United Junior Supporters' Club, then that's exactly what it's going to be. Not your own private little clique. It's open to membership to anybody, whether you like the look of their faces or whether you don't.'

In vain Boxer tried to tell him about Bernie's past. Rasputin wasn't interested in allegations of thieving, or anything else for that matter, which couldn't be proved.

'He's dead right, of course,' said Mac.

'But I'm telling you, Mac, he'll ruin everything,' wailed Boxer.

'So, if he does, *then* boot him out. Till then you haven't got a leg to stand on.'

There was nothing they could do. Bernie Russell and Scobie Beeson were members of their club.

Mac made it quite clear that he wasn't putting up any money to decorate their clubroom for them. 'I can't even afford to decorate my own office this year,' he said. But when Bernie heard the other kids discussing how they could raise money for the club, he was quick to offer his father's money – in return for a place on the committee. The others weren't having that. They'd find their own money, they said, and it was Boxer who hit upon the idea of a disco.

'We couldn't have it here, it's too yukky,' said Sheila, but Gerry said they could make a feature of it.

'We can call it a Tramps' Disco,' he said. 'Get everyone to come in their grottiest gear.'

'Great!' said Wurzel.

'Yeah, you could come as you are,' the Prof told him.

They couldn't afford a group, but Jenny thought they could get a DJ for twenty pounds. Funky Freddy Friendly had done a disco for a girl in her class at school on her birthday, and he was happy to come to Dunmore United the following Saturday. He was a tubby man, with a red satin shirt and a blond streak along one side of his dark hair. His amplifiers made the whole building rock and the disco was a wild success. Lots of kids came, punks and skinheads, and even a few soul kids, but they didn't stay long because the heavy metal music wasn't to their taste. There was no trouble though, except for Bernie and Scobie, who tried to barge in without paying.

'Who's a clever boy, then?' said Boxer, surveying with satisfaction the crowded room full of kids dancing beneath the flashing coloured lights.

'Great, isn't it?' said Gerry. 'And we've taken more than fifty quid on the door. We'll be able to get the paint now, even after paying Funky Freddy.'

But when the time came to pay him, Wurzel went to the drawer, where they had locked the evening's takings in an Oxo tin, and found to his horror that it had been forced open. The money had gone.

'Oh no, really? That's terrible,' said Freddy, when they told him. 'But er – where does that leave me, then? I mean, deepest sympathy and all that, of course. But this is my living, know what I mean?'

The kids looked at each other in consternation. Then Gerry had a brainwave. They had been selling soft drinks all evening.

'There's still the money we took on the drinks,' he said. He went over to the little bar they had set up in the corner, with Funky Freddy following close on his heels.

'What a shocking thing though, eh?' he said, as he pocketed his twenty quid with evident relief.

'Whoever could have done it?' said Sheila.

'I can think of one who might,' said Boxer, grimly. 'Two in fact.'

They looked round. Bernie and Scobie were nowhere to be seen.

Bernie saw Boxer waiting for him as he came along the tunnel by the terraces the next day, and he sensed trouble. He turned and ran, first over the terraces and then across the pitch, where Boxer felled him with a swift rugger tackle.

'I didn't take it,' he whimpered, as Boxer brought him down.

'What didn't you take?' said Boxer, holding him down. 'How d'you know anything was taken?'

But before Bernie could reply, Charlie Russell was on top of them and hurling Boxer angrily away from his son.

'Are you all right, Bernie?' he said breathlessly.

At the sight of his father, Bernie's face contorted, as if with pain. 'He booted me,' he said, clutching his ribs.

'I never touched him,' said Boxer, angrily.

'You little animal,' yelled Charlie, and was about to grab Boxer when Mac intervened.

'All right, that's enough of that,' he called from the entrance to the players' tunnel. 'What's going on?'

'He booted me,' said Bernie again.

'I never. He nicked our money –' said Boxer.

'He's lying, Dad,' said Bernie.

'Can you prove what you're saying?' Mac asked Boxer sternly.

'I'm telling you, Mac. He just admitted it.'

'But can you *prove* it?'

'No.'

'See?' said old man Russell triumphantly. 'Now, listen to me, Murphy. I want that little thug banned from the ground. As of now.'

'All right,' said Mac, raising a restraining hand to calm Charlie down. 'Leave it to me, Mr Russell.'

Charlie did not want to be calmed. He turned on Mac.

'Now look, you. Just in case it's slipped your mind, I do happen to be a director of this club.'

'And just in case it's slipped yours, Mr Russell, I do happen to be the manager.'

'Right. If you won't listen to me, perhaps there's somebody else you will listen to. Come on, Bernie.'

He marched off, a protective arm on Bernie's shoulder. Bernie walked stiffly, still clutching his ribs in dramatic illustration of the wrongs he had suffered.

'What an act,' Boxer yelled after him. 'Give him the Oscar.'

'Shut *up*,' said Mac.

'He took our money,' said Boxer, defiantly.

So far as Rasputin could see, Boxer was completely in the wrong.

'I don't agree,' Mac told him. 'If I had to choose between Bernie or Boxer, I know who my money would be on.'

'You know something?' said Rasputin, sarcastically. 'You missed your way. You should have been a probation officer, not a soccer manager.'

'I'll ask you just once more,' said Mac. 'Are you asking me to ban the kid from the ground or aren't you?'

'Oh, I dunno –' said Rasputin. To tell the truth, he didn't care much for Charlie Russell and his whingeing son either. Russell was bent as a three quid note, but the fact remained, he was still on the Board. 'I dunno,' he said again. 'You're the flaming manager. You decide. Just leave me out of it, right?'

And so, of course, Boxer was allowed to remain in the club.

With their disco money stolen, and nothing to show for it, there remained the problem of doing up the club. The Prof and Wurzel went to Rasputin, and offered to sell souvenirs for him on match days, free of charge, from the junior clubroom, but Rasputin just told them to beetle off. Then Bernie made them another offer. He'd had a word with the old man, he said. Mr Russell was prepared to let them have the paint for nothing.

'Where'd he get it from, Bernie?' said Boxer, from the other end of the clubroom. 'Fall off a lorry, did it?'

'You shouldn't say things like that. Not about his dad,' Jean told Boxer when Bernie and Scobie had left. But Boxer was unrepentant. As far as he was concerned, Bernie had taken the disco money. He didn't know how he had the neck to keep coming to the club. He loathed Bernie, and proof had nothing to do with it.

The feeling was mutual. Bernie loathed Boxer too, and he was determined to fix him once and for all. So he and Scobie waited behind at the ground until everyone had gone home. Hidden behind a buttress in the forecourt, they watched Mac lock up his offices and drive away in his battered old Jaguar. Then they stole out and forced a side door. As they made their way behind the terraces, they passed a chained and barking Rover, but there was no one to hear him.

The Social Club – Cassidy's domain – was Bernie's

target. The door was locked, but Bernie threw a brick through the window next to the door, put his arm in cautiously and freed the catch.

'What's the matter, Scobie? Going chicken on me, are you?' he said, laughing at Scobie's frightened rabbit face.

'Course not,' said Scobie, valiantly, and followed Bernie into the Social Club. It was dim in there, with no lights on, and the bar all shuttered with a metal grille.

'What now, then?' said Scobie nervously.

'I told you. We fix him good,' said Bernie. He went over to one of the fruit machines, got his weight behind it and pushed it over on its side with a crash. Next he kicked over a table.

'Come on, then,' he told the watching Scobie.

Scobie half-heartedly kicked a chair across the room. Bernie grinned. He was about to send another table flying, when he spotted the bucket of sand standing next to the piano. It was there in case of fire and a lot of people had left fag ends in it. Bernie's eyes lit up. He opened the top of the piano, and then hoisted the bucket up to his shoulder.

'What about a bit of music, then? Something from "The Desert Song" –' he said, as he tipped the sand which first thudded, and then trickled, down over the strings in the piano's innards.

Elaine discovered the damage next day. She had allowed Mac to talk her into doing his secretarial work for him, and she had gone down to the Social Club to make them both a cup of tea.

'Why would anyone want to do a thing like this?' she said to Mac, horrified at the savagery of the attack on the club.

Mac shrugged. 'Why is there violence on the terraces? Why are half the walls around the place covered with graffiti? Because the country's sick,' he said. 'Kids don't respect people's property any more. If somebody's got something you haven't got, smash it. Or scratch it, or nick it. It's pathetic.'

Rasputin, when he came in at Mac's summons, was equally disgusted.

'Mindless! Who the hell would want to do a place over like that? Just for kicks.'

'Well, that's for the police to find out,' said Cassidy, tight-lipped. The piano in his beloved Social Club was ruined, a write-off. 'But I know who my money would be on as likely candidates. If you give every little tear-away on the estate the run of the place, you shouldn't be surprised if this sort of thing happens.'

'He could have a point,' said Rasputin. 'It was some-thing your little friends went in for, not all that long ago. Kicking the place to bits.'

'I don't believe for a minute they were responsible,' said Mac loyally. 'We haven't had a spot of vandalism on the ground since we gave them their own place here.'

'Until last night, right?' said Rasputin, cynically.

He didn't recognize the voice when someone, a boy, phoned him from a call-box half an hour later.

'Mr Jones? Would you like to know who it was did your club over last night?'

'Who is that?' demanded Rasputin. Then, when there was no reply: 'Who is it?'

'I don't want to say,' said the voice. 'He might go and duff me up.'

'Who might?'

'Boxer Reed. The kid who did your club –'

'Now just hang on,' said Rasputin, but the voice wheedled on, not listening to him.

'If you want proof, well, you know those beer bottles he nicked? You'll find the empties in his dustbin.'

And then the phone went dead. Rasputin looked at it

thoughtfully. A crate of beer had gone missing last night. He went across to the ground, where Mac was training some players out on the pitch.

'Does the name Boxer Reed mean anything to you?' he asked him.

It was bad luck for Boxer that the previous evening he'd gone out on his own to the pictures. He'd been ill a couple of weeks earlier, and he'd missed the film all the others were raving about. When Mac and Rasputin came round to see his parents, his story sounded very thin. Nevertheless, as his father said, it wasn't on to make serious allegations without proof.

'Well, I think I might have some proof,' Rasputin told him, and with Mr Reed's permission he disappeared out of the back door, and a moment later came back with two empty beer bottles.

'These are yours, are they, Mr Reed?'

Boxer's father shook his head. 'I don't have beer in the house.'

'Mrs Reed?'

'Of course not.'

'Funny,' said Rasputin. ''Cos I just found them in your dustbin. Right where I'd been told I would. The beer that was knocked off last night was the same brand as these are.'

Mr Reed stared at him and then at his son.

'Don't look at me, Dad, I didn't put them there,' Boxer said. He remembered suddenly the trouble he'd been in for making accusations he couldn't prove. 'And he can't prove I did,' he shouted angrily.

'No, I can't,' said Rasputin, coldly. 'But perhaps the local fuzz can. Meanwhile don't come within a mile of my football ground ever again, son.'

'But I didn't *do* it,' shouted Boxer. He turned to Mac. 'You believe me, don't you?'

Mac shook his head. 'I'll be honest with you, son. I don't know what to believe.' He shrugged regretfully at Mr Reed and followed Rasputin out of the flat.

'Dad?' said Boxer desperately.

His father said nothing.

'I believe you, Boxer,' said Jean, quietly.

'Yeah, but they don't,' said Boxer, looking from one to the other of his parents. 'I can see they don't.'

Things were very tough for Boxer for the next few days. The police came and questioned him, and though he stuck to his story, inside he was hurting. He couldn't bear to talk about it, even to Jean.

At the club, Bernie and Scobie were taking a keen interest in what was happening to Boxer.

'Have they charged him yet?' Scobie asked Jean.

'No, they haven't,' said Jean indignantly. ''Cos he didn't do it.'

Gonk was watching Bernie carefully.

'You know, whoever rang Rasputin planted those bottles in your bin,' he said thoughtfully, when Bernie and Scobie had swaggered off.

'But why?' asked Jean.

'To get Boxer into trouble.'

'But who would want to do a thing like that?'

'I can think of somebody who might,' said Sheila. 'Somebody who'd do anything to get even with Boxer.'

Once they'd thought of the idea it seemed obvious. Of course it was Bernie. Gerry went round to see Boxer that evening and put it to him.

'Look, there were two empties in your dustbin, right?'

Boxer nodded. 'Right.'

'So what happened to the rest of the bottles? There were two dozen nicked.'

'He drank them?' suggested Boxer.

'Give over. He can't have. Not 'em all.'

38

'He's hidden them somewhere then –' Boxer snapped his fingers. 'I know. He has this boat. One his dad bought him. He moors it down on the river –'

Four of them went down to the river, Boxer, Gerry, Sheila and Jenny. Bernie's boat was a little fibreglass motor boat with a small cabin. It didn't take them very long to search it. There was no sign of the crate of beer, but what they did find was the Oxo tin, the one that had gone missing on the night of the disco. They decided to take it to Mac, and were just walking along the river bank towards the bridge when Boxer spotted Bernie and Scobie coming. They dived round the far side of the bridge, and hid behind the parapet.

'What about a quick snifter, then?' Bernie was saying to Scobie as they crossed the bridge. As usual, Scobie was lagging behind Bernie, uncertain about his schemes. He seemed reluctant about the drink. 'Give over, it'll put hairs on your skinny little chest,' said Bernie. He jumped aboard the boat and from their hiding-place the others could hear the sound of splashing, followed by a loud trickle of water running off something back into the river. Boxer peered out and saw Bernie hauling a bag made of heavy polythene, the kind they sold cement in, up over the side of the boat. He had his back to the bridge as he landed his catch with a bump on the deck; Boxer and the others took their opportunity and slipped up on to the bridge, where they had a better view.

'Nice and cool. Just how I like it,' said Bernie to Scobie, as he untied the sack and passed him a bottle of beer.

'Well, well, well,' called Boxer loudly from the bridge. 'How about that then? Having a party, are you, Bernie?'

'Can anyone come?' said Jenny.

Bernie stared up at them in dismayed astonishment.

*

The kids took the Oxo tin and the remaining bottles beer to Mac. He lined them up on his desk when Charlie Russell came to see him.

'Celebrating something, are you?' Charlie asked him, when he saw the beer bottles.

'You could say that,' said Mac. And told Charlie that they were the bottles that had been stolen from the club, and that they'd been found on his son's boat.

'I hope you're not suggesting my son was responsible?'

'No,' said Mac. 'I leave things like that to the police.'

Charlie Russell stared at him. Then he gave a quick, false laugh, and snapped his fingers.

'I've just remembered. Those aren't the bottles that were nicked from the club. They're mine. A couple of weeks ago I borrowed the boat to go fishing. I took a mate along, and we had a couple of crates of beer. They'll be what was left.'

'I see,' said Mac. 'And you left these bottles on the boat, right?'

'Right.'

'Not hidden in a plastic bag and hung over the side?'

Charlie stared at him. 'I don't know what you mean.'

'I had a funny feeling you wouldn't, somehow.'

Charlie lost his temper then. 'I've told you how those bottles got there. Now you tell me what you're doing removing them from my boat. I'll have the police on to you.'

'The phone's there,' said Mac. 'Help yourself. Only before you do – look at this.' He tossed the Oxo tin over to Charlie. 'It's the tin the kids of the Junior Supporters' Club used to keep money in.'

'It's empty,' said Charlie.

'It is now. There was fifty quid in it the night somebody nicked it from the disco they were holding. The disco your son and his mate attended, by the way. He found that on board as well.'

'Who did?'

'Boxer Reed. The kid who's been accused of smashing up the Social Club.'

'Oh well, that says it all, doesn't it?' said Charlie. 'He's just set this whole thing up – to clear himself and to blame Bernie. He probably nicked the fifty quid as well.'

'He wasn't on his own when he found it,' said Mac quietly. 'There were other kids with him. All willing to swear to what they saw.'

Charlie Russell changed his tack then. He tried to put things right in the only way he knew. He pulled out his wallet and counted five notes off a fat wad of tenners.

'There's the fifty quid, right. That squares that. Plus another ten, say, for the beer –'

'And the damage to the club?'

'The insurance is taking care of that,' said Charlie. 'They can afford it. Oh, and shall we say another hundred for yourself? To cover any personal inconvenience you may have suffered.'

Mac looked at Charlie in disbelief.

'And Boxer? The kid under suspicion?'

'Tell the police you're not pressing charges. After all, they were never able to prove he did it.'

'You know something, Mr Russell? I've got a strong stomach, but people like you make me sick. I'll take fifty for the kids. You can sort the rest out with Rasputin and the police.'

'Two hundred –' said Charlie, counting off yet more tens.

'Get out,' said Mac. He'd had enough. And when Charlie started pleading for poor Bernie he finally told Charlie what he thought: that Bernie was a spoiled vindictive brat who'd stolen, for kicks, money which other kids desperately needed. He'd smashed up the club for no other reason than to get another kid blamed for it. He suggested Charlie go home and give Bernie the thrashing he deserved.

'I'll not take that sort of talk from you, Murphy,' said Charlie. 'I'll have you out of this job in no time at all.'

Mac shook his head. 'You really think you're going to be in a position to? When Rasputin finds out who it was who really smashed up his club?'

It was a good moment for Boxer when Rasputin faced his parents and told them he'd been wrong; and a better one when he was back at the club with his mates. Best of all, Rasputin decided he was going to allow the Junior Supporters' Club to sell souvenirs on match days. And their club would be decorated after all.

Gonk was a natural athlete. He could do wonders with a football: run, dribble, shoot with either foot. When he juggled a ball, he could bounce it off his head, chest, knees or feet and keep it in the air till the count reached three, or even sometimes four thousand. When Derek Cassidy saw him doing this one day in the gym, he stopped and asked his name and what school he went to; the following Saturday he and Rasputin were on the touchline, watching Gonk score three goals.

Mac was also aware of Gonk's talents. The kids had dragged him along to the first school match of the season.

'What do you think of him?' they'd asked excitedly when Gonk scored his second goal that match.

'Not bad,' Mac had said cannily. Privately he thought the kid was the best prospect of his age he had seen for a very long time.

'Ever thought of turning pro?' he asked the boy.

Gonk grinned and shook his head. He told Mac he wanted to be a vet.

'Wise lad,' said Mac. 'I wish I'd had the sense to train for a proper career when I was your age.' He meant it. At Gonk's age he'd set his heart on being a professional footballer and it had never occurred to him that he wouldn't be a top-flight player. At twenty-five he'd realized he wasn't going to make it, and there was nothing else he could do. That was when he'd gone into football management.

If Mac was content to leave Gonk to follow his own ambitions, Rasputin was not.

'When I was his age I wanted to be a flamin' astronaut,' he told Mac. 'I say we have another go at him.'

'We couldn't sign him yet, even if he was willing,' said Mac. 'He's only thirteen.'

'We could do what everybody else does,' said Rasputin. 'Have him down here for training. And by the time his fourteenth birthday rolls round we'll be the first in the queue, won't we?'

'I don't think we should,' said Mac. 'If a kid has his sights set on something else, I don't believe it's right for us to interfere.'

'He can always say no.'

'He already has.'

'To you, Mac,' said Rasputin. 'Not to me.'

The clubhouse was newly painted, and Wurzel was just putting the finishing touches to what he insisted on calling his 'mur-i-al' – because in the midst of all his jagged psychedelic shapes there was a rather sinister mauve eye – when Rasputin bounced in.

'Hi kids, how's it going?' he said cheerfully.

'We should be ready for Saturday's match,' Sheila told him.

'Good,' said Rasputin, still moving across the room. He stopped at Gonk, who was squatting down, painting a skirting-board.

'You'll be Gary Roberts, right?' he said.

Gonk nodded.

'Got a minute, have you?' said Rasputin, and whisked Gonk off to his office at the roller rink, leaving the other kids to speculate what it was he wanted.

'Sit down, don't look so worried,' Rasputin said

affably. Gonk sat down rather awkwardly on the edge of one of Rasputin's leather chairs. His hands were painty and it bothered him. He was worried he was going to get paint on Mr Jones's plush furnishings.

'Great game you had on Saturday morning,' said Rasputin. 'How many d'you get in the end? Two, was it?'

'Three,' said Gonk.

'I'll be frank with you, kid,' said Rasputin. 'I've made a lot of bread in my time. A lot. But I'd swap the lot for what you've got in your feet. Have you ever thought of turning pro?'

'No.'

'You're potty,' said Rasputin. 'Do you realize how much top footballers make these days? You could be a millionaire.'

'I'd rather be a vet,' said Gonk.

Rasputin shrugged. 'So be a pro footballer first and make your bread – and use it to set yourself up as a vet. Look, I tell you what we'll do. Let's forget all about whether you want to turn pro or not. But every night after school during the season you come down to the ground and train with us, all right? See then how you feel about it.'

But Gonk couldn't do that. He worked at the vet's every night for experience. Rasputin looked at Gonk in exasperation. Most kids would give their right arm for a chance such as he was offering the kid. He opened a drawer in his desk and took out an envelope which he tossed casually across his desk to the boy.

'Open it,' he said.

Gonk did so, and boggled at the wad of bank notes inside.

'You know how much you're holding in your hand, son? Two thousand pounds. Just think how much that is. And it's yours. Free, gratis and for nothing. If we have a gentleman's agreement – me and your dad – that when you turn fourteen, you sign schoolboy forms for us.'

For a second Gonk said nothing. He was thinking how much the money would mean to his parents. Then he stood up.

'I've told you, Mr Jones, I'm not interested. I'm just not. I have to go now. Thanks for asking me, like.' And he opened the door carefully, so as not to get paint on the handle, and let himself out of Rasputin's office.

Never one to take no for an answer, Rasputin decided to repeat his offer to Gonk's parents, and that evening saw the Rolls drawing up outside the Roberts's flat on the council estate, with Rasputin and Cassidy inside it.

'Not exactly Park Lane,' said Rasputin.

'His old fellow's on the dole,' said Cassidy. 'Made redundant about a year ago. Hasn't been able to get a job since – which can't be bad news for you, Mr Jones.'

Gonk's father was a gentle, dignified West Indian, who turned out to be as immovable as his son. He sent his wife to make a cup of tea while he heard Rasputin out.

'I say it to you, and I'll say it to all the others who'll be coming after you before he's very much older,' he said. 'It's his life and his decision. Not mine or his mother's.' And he handed back Rasputin's envelope, seemingly as unimpressed as his son had been by the cash offer, which Rasputin had upped by five hundred pounds.

Still Rasputin did not give up. He thought of a new way to put pressure on Gonk. His dad was out of work, right? Well, not only would he hand over the two thousand five hundred, but he would offer Mr Roberts a job at his roller rink.

He had found Gonk's weak spot. Gonk knew how much his father hated being out of work, how soul-destroying he found it, hanging about the house all day. Besides, as Rasputin kept on at him, it began to seem to him that he was being pigheaded and selfish in seeking to be a vet. It would mean he wouldn't earn for a long time, that his parents would have to support him through the long years of study. Whereas if he became a footballer, in a year or two he might be able to support them ...

'I'm going to go down the club of a night time after school,' he told his parents the day he decided.

'But you always go to the vet's,' said his mother.

'I'm sick of the vet's. I'm just cheap labour to them. Anyway, I'd rather play football.' He took the envelope out of his pocket and gave it to his father.

'It's for you and Mum. There's two and a half thousand quid in there.'

'No thanks,' said his dad. 'Anyway, it's an illegal payment.'

'Who cares?' said Gonk.

'I care.'

He refused to take it but in the end he agreed to hold the money for Gonk.

Mac knew Rasputin must have been up to something, though what he didn't know, when he heard Gonk was coming.

'Look, Mac, what's the matter with you?' said Rasputin, who couldn't understand Mac's scruples. 'In a few years when he's running out on to the Wembley turf with an English shirt on his back and a hundred thousand people chanting for him he'll bless the day he met me.'

For the time being, however, it was quite clear Gonk was *not* blessing Rasputin. He turned up for training sure enough, but it was a dutiful appearance, as if all the joy had gone out of the game for him. The truth was, he felt cornered. He'd taken the payment, and worse, his father had taken the job, and now he had to come, and he hated it. It showed in the way he played. Rasputin, watching his new investment, was furious.

'What's the matter with him?' he grumbled from the touchline. 'He's doing nothing out there.'

Mac understood. 'The kid's heart isn't in it any more,' he said.

'Well, you're the manager,' said Rasputin. 'Talk to him about it. 'Cos just for the record, I've got two and a half grand invested in that kid already.'

It was the first Mac had heard of it, and he couldn't believe his ears.

'You what?'

'You heard. Or rather, you didn't hear,' said Rasputin.

'Great. *Great*,' said Mac grimly to himself, when he thought about Rasputin's illegal deal. He tried to awaken some enthusiasm in Gonk's game, but the kid remained wooden and depressed.

There was only one thing about Dunmore United which could still bring a smile to Gonk's face, and that was Rover. The dog was allowed to wander loose about the ground now, and one day he was chasing a cat when he rushed out into the street right under the wheels of a passing car. There was a screech of brakes and a chilling yelp from the dog, and Gonk was on the scene in seconds. He carried the dog, whose leg was badly smashed, up to the Junior Supporters' Club where, with the kids and Mac and Elaine all quietly watching, he laid the dog out on a table. Boxer almost threw up when he saw the damaged leg, but Gonk was cool and competent. He washed and bound it, talking quietly to the dog all the while to soothe him. Mac and Elaine exchanged a look at his confidence and expertise.

'Right, that should hold it till we get down to the vet's,' he said when he'd finished. Mac stepped forward to lift the animal, but Rover wasn't having it. He wanted Gonk.

'Has he always been that good with animals?' asked Elaine, as she helped the other kids clear away the blood and dirty swabs.

'Oh yeah, terrific,' said Gerry. 'He wants to be a vet. Well – he used to,' he added awkwardly.

'Doesn't he still? Really?' said Elaine shrewdly. 'How did Mr Jones get him to change his mind?'

'You'd better ask him, Mrs Murphy,' said Gerry, embarrassed.

'I'm asking you.'

'It was his dad.'

'His dad's idea?'

'No – Gonk's dad's been out of work for ages. Rasputin offered to fix him up with a job, like. If he said he'd sign.'

'Well, well, well,' said Mac, when Elaine told him about it later. 'And there was me, thinking it was the money that had turned his head.'

'I think it's disgusting,' said Elaine. 'Playing on a boy's family loyalty like that. What are you going to do about it?'

'Me? What can I do? If they've done a deal, what the hell can I do about it?'

'You've got to do something, Mac. For your own sake.'

'What do you mean?'

'If that boy's heart isn't in it now, it never will be. Which means that within a couple of years Rasputin will have given up on him and thrown him out. With no qualifications to speak of and no chance of picking up his studies where he left off. And if you've been a party to that –' Elaine was passionate – 'well, you'll be nearly as much to blame as Rasputin.'

She was right, of course, and Mac knew it. He went to see Mr Roberts that same day and told him about his own faded unrealized ambitions. The next day Gonk's dad was in Rasputin's office returning the envelope stuffed with notes. Rasputin was furious.

'Who's got at you?' he wanted to know.

'Nobody's got at us, Mr Jones,' said Mr Roberts, with quiet dignity. 'We've changed our minds, that's all.'

'I don't suppose for a minute you had anything to do with it?' said Rasputin, eyeing Mac suspiciously later that morning.

'Me? I haven't said a word to the kid. Why would I?' said Mac, innocently. 'Am I really in a position to discourage potential talent with the playing staff I'm lumbered with?'

'Let's put it this way. I sincerely hope not,' said Rasputin.

Though the next week, when he saw Mr Roberts working alongside old Sam Fletcher as a groundsman, he knew Mac had had a hand in it after all. Mac didn't mind. It was worth it to see Gonk happy. He was working at the vet's again and his game was back to its usual brilliance, now that he knew it was only a game once more.

The first home match of the season, the kids were to sell
souvenirs from their redecorated clubroom, as they'd
agreed with Rasputin. The Friday beforehand they all
spent the evening in the clubroom. The boys were about
their usual pursuits, the Prof reading, oblivious of the
music blaring from the speakers, Gonk and Boxer playing
table tennis, Gerry throwing darts. Rover the dog
wandered among them, his splinted leg still in bandages.
It was the girls who were busy preparing for the shop
that was to operate from the clubroom next day. Jean
unpacked a large cardboard carton of club scarves which
had been delivered that afternoon, and Sheila made out
a neat rota of who was to be on duty.

'Hey, are they new?' called Gerry, as he spotted Dunmore's colours emerging from the box.

'Yeah. On sale for the first time tomorrow,' said Jean.

'How much?'

'Two quid.'

'Can I take one now?' Gerry lifted one of the scarves
and hooked it round his neck. 'I'll pay you at the match
tomorrow.'

'All right,' said Jean, and Gerry wandered off to see
what Sheila was pinning to the noticeboard.

It was the rota. Gerry looked at it curiously. At the
last committee meeting they'd all agreed that at least one
boy and one girl should be on shop duty at all home

matches. As this would mean they'd miss most of the match that day, they'd agreed to do it by turns.

'Hey, hang about, Sheel,' said Gerry, seeing his name at the top of the list. 'According to this I'm on tomorrow.'

'Well, somebody has to be on.'

'Yeah, but why me?'

'Well, for one thing, you are club secretary. And for another –' she grinned disarmingly – 'well, I've put myself on for tomorrow. And I thought you'd like to be with me.'

Gerry was not won over. 'You might at least have asked me,' he grumbled.

'If I went round asking,' said Sheila, 'nobody'd want to do tomorrow, would they? Not the first match.'

'So I end up doing it. Terrific.'

'With me, though,' Sheila pointed out. She was hurt that this didn't appear to make the slightest difference to Gerry.

Boxer, beaten hollow by Gonk once more, wandered over then and wanted to know what they were arguing about.

'Somebody has to be first, mate,' he backed up Sheila.

'Yes, but why *me*?'

'I've told you why,' said Sheila. 'You're just being stupid.'

'I'll tell you what's stupid,' said Gerry. 'It's this shop idea. That's stupid. Well, thanks, Sheila. Thanks a bunch.' And with that he stalked out of the room. Sheila went running after him.

'Where are you going?' she demanded.

'Home.'

'Just for that?'

''Cos I want to.'

'And what about me? Who's going to walk me home?'

'Try Boxer,' said Gerry, crossly. 'You and him seem dead cosy all of a sudden.' It was unfair and he knew it, but he didn't care. Let Sheila have a bad day over it. She shouldn't have made him miss tomorrow's match.

Saturday came and the ground seemed unexpectedly lively and busy, as if the word of Mac's arrival had put new spirit into Dunmore's demoralized supporters. A new club flag was flying from the masthead, and there were queues at the gate. Rasputin gave an interview to a couple of local newspaper reporters.

'Never better,' he said of the club's prospects for the coming season. 'I think we're going to surprise quite a lot of people round here.'

'What are your feelings about violence on the terraces?' the reporter asked him next.

'Very strong feelings, actually,' said Rasputin. 'We'll tolerate no louts here at United. From now on, any fan of ours guilty of causing trouble is banned from this club. For life.'

It was unfortunate he should have said this in an interview, as things were to turn out that day.

In the junior clubroom Sheila and Jenny, with Wurzel and Boxer, had set up a stall at one end and laid out all the scarves, pennants and photographs on it. Sheila hadn't heard from Gerry since he walked out the previous evening, and she was twitchy. Every time the door opened she looked up expectantly, hoping it would be him. This time she looked up, it was a kid with long hair in a grubby denim jacket. He wore the colours of the visiting team. He came over to the stall and looked over the stuff. Sheila looked anxiously at her watch. Gerry should have been here by now. Perhaps he was so angry he wasn't coming.

'He'll come,' said Jenny, sensing her anxiety. 'Don't worry.' She was keeping an eye on the long-haired kid.

He noticed. 'What are you looking at, then?' he said aggressively.

'Not a lot,' said Jenny, who was not easily intimidated.

'Funny girl,' said the long-haired kid menacingly. Wurzel looked up from across the room and nudged Boxer. Boxer strolled over.

'Want something, do you?'

'What's it to you?'

'On your bike,' said Boxer. The boy glared at him but, realizing he was outnumbered, did as he was told. As he turned to go, they saw that he had Black Sabbath embroidered across the back of his jacket. They were to see that again before the day was out.

A roar from the crowd outside told them that the players were taking the field. Gerry had still not appeared.

'You go, Jenny,' said Sheila. 'I'll be fine on my own, honest.'

'No, I'll stay with you,' said Jenny. 'I hate football, anyway.'

'You hate it?' Wurzel was surprised. 'Why do you come here, then?'

'The boys. What else?' said Jenny. Which was honest of her, because it was Wurzel she fancied. 'Well, go on, then,' she added, as they heard the ref's whistle. 'You'll miss the kick-off.'

And so the boys went. As they ran down the corridor, the girls could hear them yelling hoarsely, 'Up United!'

It was an exciting match. United put one in, in the first five minutes, and then seemed to forget they still had another eighty-five minutes of play. Their opponents kept the ball up their end, while Mac bit his nails and cursed first one of his defenders and then another. Then United's keeper made a sensational save, a ball slicing in at such an angle it seemed impossible, and after that United regained their form, and by half-time they were two–nil up.

Jenny and Sheila were still on their own in the clubroom, with no sign of Gerry, when the long-haired kid in the Black Sabbath jacket arrived back with reinforcements, about six of his mates. First they all demanded cokes from the refreshment counter.

'Sorry, members only,' said Jenny, firmly.

Next they started messing about with the souvenirs. 'How much for this, darlin'? Two quid? It's bigger rubbish than your team.'

'Is that why we're winning then?' Jenny asked them.

The Black Sabbath kid picked up a framed photograph of the United goalkeeper.

'Breakable is it, this glass?' he said.

'Put it down,' said Jenny.

'Make me,' challenged the kid.

'Right,' said Jenny. Although she was a small girl, she wasn't in the least afraid of Black Sabbath, who was thin and rather weedy. As she went after him, he tossed the photograph to one of the other kids. Jenny stamped hard on his foot and made a dive for the other boy, who threw it on to a third. By this time all their mates were throwing souvenirs around, while Sheila helplessly tried to clutch as many things as she could. The place was in chaos when Boxer and the others arrived. They took one look at what was happening and then laid into the visiting supporters. Within minutes Mac had a mini-riot in his club.

When Gerry arrived, damp-haired and breathless, at the ground a quarter of an hour later he was astonished to see about fifteen kids being loaded into a police van, and even more amazed to see Wurzel, Boxer, Gonk and Jenny among them. He couldn't imagine what had happened, but there was no time to ask, for the doors of the van slammed shut and the van drove off. Gerry hurried up to the junior clubroom where he found Sheila, pale and tearful, picking up the pieces in the devastation.

'What the hell's happened?' he asked her.

'They've all been arrested, that's what's happened,' said Sheila bitterly. 'And it's all your fault, Gerry Jackson.'

'My fault?' said Gerry. 'I wasn't even here.'

'Exactly,' said Sheila. 'If you had been, they might not have tried anything on. Only you weren't here, were you? You were too busy sulking.'

'Hang on a minute, let me explain –' said Gerry. But Sheila wasn't prepared to listen. Nor did she think to ask why Gerry's hair was plastered damply over his head in the middle of a Saturday afternoon. Instead she spent the next few days aching with miserable anger and hating Gerry for letting them all down.

Mac was livid when he heard what had happened. Once again in his eyes the kids had betrayed him. Cassidy was grinning to himself in silent triumph, Rasputin was dancing with rage and saying – again – that they were never to be allowed on his premises, and so it fell to Elaine to go down to the police station and sort matters out. When it was explained what had happened, the United supporters were not charged and Rasputin agreed, reluctantly, to give them yet another chance.

All did not end well for everyone, however. When Jenny's father saw her bruised face, she was forbidden to come to the club any more. The brawl had confirmed his worst fears that the Junior Supporters' Club was just a bunch of hooligans. And when Gerry came to the club to pay the two pounds he owed for the scarf, Wurzel and Boxer told him they thought he was the cause of the trouble. If he'd been there, the fight would never have started.

'I reckon you owe us an explanation,' said Wurzel.

'Do you?' said Gerry.

'So do we get one or don't we?' said Wurzel.

'I got held up,' said Gerry.

'By what?'

'None of your business,' said Gerry.

'Well, what sort of answer's that?' said Sheila.

'All you're going to get,' said Gerry. 'Take it or leave it.' And as the others all started to protest: 'And if any of you are thinking of trying to kick me out – don't bother, 'cos I've just resigned.'

With that he walked out, to be followed by the Prof and Gonk, who said they were resigning with him.

'So who needs them? Who needs them?' said Wurzel airily.

'Just shut up, Wurzel, will you?' said Sheila. 'Shut up. Just for once.' As far as she was concerned the club might as well not exist any more.

When Jenny Lee's father said she wasn't to go down to the
club ever again, he meant it. He was quite an elderly
father, in his fifties, a widower, and rather staid. He
thought that children these days were given far too much
freedom and made strict rules for Jenny. She had to be in
when he said, and he had absolutely forbidden her to
have her ears pierced. Jenny minded this. All kids had
their ears pierced these days, boys and girls.

She wasn't seen in the club the following week, and
neither was Gerry, though Gerry saw something of the
place when he did his paper round, because Mac had his
papers delivered to the club. He saw something of Wurzel
too, because the Lees were also on his round, and Wurzel
was forever hanging about outside the Lees' house in the
hope of seeing Jenny. Gerry and he weren't speaking.
They just glared at each other.

Mr Lee noticed Wurzel that week as well. Wurzel was
everything of which he disapproved – he was scruffy and
he slouched on street corners. He wondered why he was
watching the house all the time, and when he saw Jenny
talking to him on her way home from school he summoned her inside immediately.

'I've told you, you're to keep away from boys like that,'
he told her, as he shut the front door.

'I can't just ignore him,' said Jenny. 'Anyway, what's wrong with him?'

'I would have thought that was obvious,' said Mr Lee, primly. 'Just look at him.'

'Lots of kids dress dead sloppy these days,' said Jenny. 'You're so old-fashioned, Dad.'

She slung her school bag down on a chair, but this was another thing her father felt strongly about.

'In your bedroom, if you don't mind,' he said.

Jenny sighed ostentatiously and picked it up.

'Oh, and somebody called Beryl phoned for you,' he said.

'Beryl?' said Jenny, puzzled. Then she remembered. 'Oh, yeah. Right,' she said.

When The Law, in the shape of PC Morris, walked into Mac's office that week, Mac thought at first it might be more hassle about the fight the previous Saturday. But no. PC Morris produced one of United's new-style scarves and asked Mac if he knew who it belonged to. Apparently a little girl had fallen into the canal that same Saturday, and had been fished out by a boy who'd vanished as soon as some adults had appeared and taken charge of the child.

'We'd like to get in touch with the boy,' said Morris. 'The boss would like to put him up for an award.'

'OK,' said Mac. 'Leave it with me.'

That evening he wandered into the Junior Supporters' Club. He was surprised at how few kids were there. Half the regulars seemed to be missing.

'Quiet tonight, isn't it?' he said to Sheila.

'It is a bit,' said Sheila. She was looking glum.

'Everything all right?' Mac asked her.

'Course,' said Sheila, though she didn't sound very convinced.

'Much damage done on Saturday, was there?' said Mac.

'Not really. It looked worse than it was, really.'

Mac produced the scarf. 'These went on sale for the first time Saturday, right?'

Sheila nodded.

'Sell many, did you?'

'A couple.'

'You wouldn't happen to know who to?'

Sheila did remember. A couple of girls had bought them, and the only other one was the one she'd sold to Gerry.

'Our Gerry?'

'Yeah.'

'You don't say,' said Mac. 'What time will Gerry be getting in tonight?'

'I don't think he will be,' said Sheila miserably.

'I thought he came down here most nights?'

'Not any more,' said Sheila. And then, with a bit of prodding from Mac, she told him the whole story.

'Did he say why he didn't turn up?' said Mac when she had finished.

'I didn't really give him a chance to, I was so mad at him. So he just stormed out. He hasn't been in since. Well – just once. To say he was finished with the club. Why d'you want him, anyway?'

'Oh, nothing very important, really. I just want to ask him something, that's all.'

He didn't get a chance to see Gerry for a day or two, and in the meanwhile Gerry, Gonk and the Prof hung around the streets and the children's playground getting progressively more bored.

'So – go on down the club, what's stopping you?' Gerry challenged the other two. He felt bad that they were staying away for him. They were the ones who had found the table tennis table, and now they were stuck outside with nothing to do while Boxer's lot got the benefit of it.

'We're doing it for you,' said Gonk, loyally.

'Look, I'm finished with that place, right? But that doesn't mean you shouldn't go. I mean, you're dying to, aren't you? Admit it.'

Gonk and the Prof exchanged a look. 'Come with us,' the Prof suggested cautiously to Gerry.

'No thanks,' said Gerry, and cycled off.

'What do you think?' the Prof asked Gonk.

Gonk shrugged. 'I could use a game of table tennis,' he said.

They were not the only ones to return to the club that evening. Jenny, too, appeared briefly, looking for Wurzel. She seemed worried about something. Sheila was pleased to see them all, although the person she was aching to see was Gerry, and he didn't show up.

Jenny had a blazing row with her father that night. She had told him she was going round to Mary White's house and, unfortunately for her, Mary White phoned while she was out. Her father confronted her with this fact when she came in.

'You've been to that club, haven't you?' he said, quiet with anger.

'I only called in for a minute. I was looking for somebody.'

Mr Lee guessed at once that it was Wurzel. 'That boy? Was that who you were looking for?'

'Yes,' said Jenny, defiantly. 'Why not? He's not some kind of monster, you know.'

'You can go to your room now, Jennifer,' said Mr Lee. He was still quiet and still absolutely in charge. Suddenly Jenny exploded.

'Oh, why don't you ever *listen* to me? I'm not a baby any more. I'm thirteen years old. But whenever I try to explain anything to you, all you ever say is, go up to your room.'

And now her father's anger flared. 'I'll tell you this, my girl. I'm certainly not going to sit here and listen to your cheek.'

'You see,' said Jenny. 'You *won't* listen.'

'Do as you're told,' shouted Mr Lee. And sat down, his heart beating as he tried to control his anger.

'Working for a living now, then?' said Mac, when at last he saw Gerry on his paper round again.

'Yeah,' said Gerry.

'How are you?'

'Fine,' said Gerry. He wasn't keen to hang about.

'Before you go,' said Mac, sensing this. 'This yours?' He produced the scarf. 'You did lose one, didn't you? Over the weekend?'

Gerry nodded.

'Just down by the canal bank, right? Where that kid was pulled out of the water, Saturday. By person or persons unknown.'

'Where did you get it?'

'Police brought it round. They're trying to trace the owner. They reckon by doing what he did he probably booked himself a passage to Buckingham Palace to meet the Duke of Edinburgh.' And, as Gerry was still taking this in: 'Cold was it? In the water?'

'Freezing,' said Gerry.

'Why the hell did you go running off like that? Without even letting anyone know who you were?'

'I was soaked to the skin – and, anyway, I was late.'

'Late for what?' asked Mac, though he knew perfectly well.

So Gerry told him about his shop duty, and how if he didn't turn up he knew the others would think he'd done it on purpose, and how when he'd got home his mum had insisted he had a hot bath, so he had been late after all.

'Why didn't you explain to the others?'

'I tried to,' said Gerry. 'They'd already made up their minds I'd let them down.'

Mac felt sorry for the kid. 'Would you like me to explain it to them?'

'No,' said Gerry, vehemently. 'If that's all they think of me, they can keep their rotten club.'

After that, Mac felt he couldn't interfere, although he could see Gerry was cutting off his nose to spite his face. Elaine however, when she heard the story, felt no such inhibitions. She told Sheila what had happened, and the next morning Sheila was up early and waiting for Gerry outside the newsagent's. Gerry was gruff when he saw her, so she plunged straight in.

'I think it was very brave what you did.'

'Who told you?' said Gerry, furious. 'I told Mac not to say anything.'

Sheila explained it was Elaine, not Mac. 'Anyway, why didn't you tell me?' she asked him.

''Cos you never gave me a chance, did you?'

'Sorry,' said Sheila.

But Gerry wasn't ready to forgive her, not yet.

'Come back to the club,' Sheila pleaded. 'Everyone wants you to.'

'No thanks,' said Gerry. He was too proud. He wasn't going back to the club after saying he wouldn't.

In the meantime, something much more alarming had happened at the club. Jenny Lee had gone missing. She just didn't come home from school one day. The police came to Mac to find out who her friends were, and Mac put them on to Wurzel, whose own dad was a copper. Wurzel was got out of bed in the middle of a wet and stormy night and asked if Jenny had ever talked of running away. Did he know where she might have gone? She hadn't, and Wurzel didn't, but he did have some opinions about her father having driven her to it.

'That's enough of that, Willie,' said his father. 'At the moment the man's worried to death in case something's happened to the child.'

At that particular moment, Jenny was hidden in a hedge, soaking wet and too frightened to go home. She had had her ears pierced by Beryl, a girl at school, who did it with a darning needle. She had had no idea how much it would hurt. Beryl didn't use any anaesthetic, and she hadn't sterilized the needle either. Jenny's ears were throbbing, and she was very bedraggled when finally she hit upon the idea of taking shelter in the Junior Supporters' Club. She let herself in with the key she held as a committee member, and, being careful to leave no traces, she let herself out again in the morning.

She did this for four nights, getting more frightened all the while. Her ears, instead of getting better, were getting worse. They turned into hubs of burning pain; just to touch them made her feel quite sick and faint. She didn't know what she was going to do.

In the end it was Gerry who heard her moving when he came to deliver Mac's early morning paper. She tried to run away from him, but he guessed who it was and went after her.

'Your dad's worried sick about you,' he told her. 'He went on the telly last night, asking you to come home. Go home, Jenny.'

'I daren't,' said Jenny, close to tears.

'He'll just be glad to see you,' said Gerry. Then, as she began to cry, he noticed her ears.

'What on earth have you done to them?' he said. 'They've gone septic. You'd better get to hospital. Come on, I'll get Mac.'

Of course, Mr Lee was too relieved to see Jenny safe to be angry with her. Father and daughter hugged one another in the hospital casualty cubicle. Mr Lee had had a few days to ponder what had gone wrong between the two of them, and when Wurzel came round later that day to see how Jenny was, he not only allowed him in to see Jenny but even made them all a cup of tea.

Wurzel was grateful to Gerry and that evening he was down at the newsagent's looking for him.

'Need any help, do you?' he said, watching Gerry pump up his back tyre.

'No thanks.'

'Thanks for helping Jenny.'

'Is she all right?'

'Yeah. So –' Wurzel hesitated. He was almost as bad at swallowing his pride as Gerry himself. 'See you down at the club tonight, eh? Give you a thrashing at the old table tennis.'

And, this time, Gerry wasn't too proud to go back.

Mac was out on the pitch with his squad, putting them through a series of short sharp sprints and turns, when Rasputin called him upstairs to the office to tell him the good news: Luigi Vincenti, the owner of an Italian club, had been in touch with him.

'The word is he has even more bread than I have,' crowed Rasputin.

Elaine raised her eyebrows at Sheila, who was helping her to stamp some envelopes.

'The mind boggles,' said Mac. 'What's he to us?'

'He's got this football club. Over in Italy. He reckons that when he's finished with them they'll be another Inter-Milan. And he's looking for fixtures. Friendlies. Against English clubs.'

'Us?' said Mac, disbelievingly. 'They'll slaughter us.'

'Don't think so,' said Rasputin. 'See, they're no Inter-Milan yet. Vincenti's just taken them over.'

'Oh, I see,' said Mac. This Vincenti sounded almost as modest as Rasputin himself. He winked at Elaine. 'You want me to fly over, do you? Fix up the details?'

'No need,' said Rasputin. 'He's coming over here tomorrow to set the whole thing up personally. In time to catch Saturday's game with Athletic. I've arranged to pick him up at Sutton.' Sutton was a private airfield a few miles away. 'He's got his own plane. Flies it himself.'

'I see,' said Mac. 'And just where was he thinking of staging this game with us. Over here or over there?'

'Both. It'll be a two-leg job. Just like the real thing.'

'Can't be bad,' said Mac.

With Sheila in on the news, it wasn't long before the Junior Supporters' Club heard all about it. Sam Fletcher was in the clubroom when she told them. He often came in for a cup of tea these days.

'Eye-ties now, eh?' he said, dipping a biscuit in his tea.

'Pardon?' said Sheila.

'Eye-ties,' said Sam again. 'Italians. That's what us tommies used to call 'em in the war. Eye-ties.'

'That would be the Boer War, would it, Sam?' said Wurzel innocently.

'Don't be so bloomin' cheeky,' said Sam. 'A desert rat, I was. I got me knees brown all right. Till I got captured.'

'You got captured?' Sheila couldn't imagine the stiff, elderly Sam having adventures like they saw in war movies.

'At Tobruk,' said Sam. 'By the Eye-ties.'

'Were you in a prison camp, then?' Gerry wanted to know.

'Two years,' said Sam. Then he added proudly, 'They couldn't hold old Sam, though. Oh no. First chance I got, over the wire and away.'

Sheila was fascinated. 'What did you do? When you got out?'

'Lived off the land,' said Sam. 'Travelled only at night. Then – over the mountains and into Switzerland.'

'Gosh,' said Sheila, impressed.

'Iti's. They couldn't hold old Sam. No sir.' And he swallowed the last of his tea, set the mug down on the table, and marched out.

'Imagine that,' said Wurzel. 'Old Sam a war hero. And we still won.'

Boxer was the only one of the kids who wasn't excited by the arrival of the Italians, and that was because he was in the middle of a family drama all of his own. His father, who had been on short-time for over a year, had been offered a new job as a joiner. At first Boxer was delighted.

'Terrific. When do you start?'

'Well, as soon as I've sorted out visas, passports, that sort of thing.'

'Passports?' said Boxer.

'It's a job abroad, Boxer,' said his mother, gently. 'Your dad's been offered a two-year contract on this big construction job in Kuwait. He'll make a lot of money.'

'I see,' said Boxer. 'And we're all going too, are we?'

'Oh yes. I wouldn't like to see your dad going off for two years on his own –'

'Something wrong, son?' said Mr Reed, noticing the expression on his son's face.

'No, no,' said Boxer. And took himself off to his room to think about it.

At the club, the others thought it would be interesting to go to the Middle East.

'For a holiday, maybe. Not for two years,' said Boxer.

'Least they play football out there,' said Gerry.

'United are my team,' said Boxer. 'Who wants to watch a bunch of Arabs? Probably won't even be able to say their names properly.'

'Does your dad know you don't want to go?'

Boxer shook his head. He was trying to hide his feelings from his parents. Times had been hard for a long time, and now his dad was so chuffed, he couldn't possibly tell him how he felt. He'd just have to put up with it.

Mac went with Rasputin to meet Vincenti's trim little executive jet when it flew into Sutton airfield next day. As the plane taxied to a standstill, Rasputin drove the Rolls on to the tarmac alongside it. Rasputin was looking particularly dapper and well-heeled, but Luigi Vincenti was even more elegant when he descended from the plane. He was a handsome man in his late thirties, smartly dressed, and laden with gold rings and bracelets. With him he had a hulking, impassive man he introduced as Angelo – 'my minder'.

'In my country I'm afraid if you have as much money as I have, he is something of a necessity,' he said. He complimented Rasputin on his Rolls. 'I have one myself,' he said. 'But I prefer my Lamborghinis.'

When they reached the club he seemed – predictably – unimpressed. The only thing which aroused his enthusiasm was Rover.

'Is that your dog?' he asked Gonk, who, as usual, was playing with the animal.

Gonk explained that it was Rasputin's.

'Is it safe for me to stroke him?'

'You'll be all right so long as I'm here,' said Gonk.

'Fierce then, is he?' said Luigi. The idea seemed to amuse him.

'He can be,' said Gonk. He took hold of the dog's collar to be on the safe side.

Rasputin appeared as Luigi was fussing the dog.

'I'd watch him if I were you, Luigi. He'd have you as soon as look at you.'

That night Rasputin threw a party for his Italian guests in the boardroom of the club to celebrate the deal he had set up. The first game was to be in England in March, the second in Italy in April. All the directors were there, and Mac, much against his will – there was a match he'd rather have been watching on the telly – with Elaine in a dress she'd bought specially for the occasion. After the toasts were over, and with Rasputin in an expansive mood, Luigi approached him with a surprising request. That dog of Rasputin's – he would like to buy him.

'In my country, guard dogs of quality are at a premium. I use them all of the time on my estate,' he explained.

'Well, he is something of a club mascot,' said Rasputin.

And then, because he was feeling mellow after all the cocktails he'd been drinking: 'But look, I'll give him to you.'

'No, no. I am more than happy to pay for him.'

'I'm telling you, mate, it's a gift. From me to you.'

'In that case, I accept,' said Luigi, with a brilliant smile. 'Thank you.'

Elaine, who had overheard the conversation, was mystified as to why Luigi should want a dog from England, and more than a little concerned about how Gonk would take the news. Even the thick-skinned Rasputin seemed a little awkward about it next day. He summoned Gonk to Mac's office.

'There'll be somebody calling later on this morning to pick up Rover,' he said.

'Pick him up?'

'Yeah. Take him away.'

'But why?' said Gonk.

''Cos he's theirs, now, that's why.' He deliberately avoided Gonk's eyes, which were full of hurt disbelief.

'But he can't do that – he's the club mascot.'

'So we'll get ourselves another mascot. Perhaps a billy-goat next time. Look, he's just a dog, kid. The world's full of dogs. Most of them unwanted.'

'Not to me, he's not,' said Gonk, fiercely.

'But then he isn't your dog, son, is he?' said Rasputin. Embarrassment was making him angry now. 'He's mine. And I'm telling you, I've just given him away to somebody.'

'Would you sell him to me, Mr Jones, please?' said Gonk, with quiet desperation. 'I'll ask my dad for the money –'

'Look,' exploded Rasputin. 'Can't you get it through your head? He's already gone. Been given away. Now that's it, all right?' It clearly wasn't, so he tried another tack. 'Look, it's not as if he isn't going to a good home.

He's off to be a guard dog. On this big posh Italian estate. He'll probably be scoffing fillet steaks most of the time.'

There was a moment's silence, as Gonk looked at Rasputin with lacerating reproach. Then he turned and went out of the room.

'Well, strewth,' said Rasputin. 'I mean, you let 'em take your dog for a walk, a couple of times, and all of a sudden they flaming well own him.'

But there was no sympathy coming his way from Mac or Elaine.

Angelo came for the dog later that morning. Rover growled when he reached for him, and Gonk had to put his lead on and calm him before he handed him over. The other kids couldn't think of anything to do or say that would comfort Gonk.

Then old Sam appeared for his mid-morning cup of tea. He'd seen Angelo and Luigi with the dog, and he knew what had happened. In fact, he knew more than the kids, for he'd heard them congratulating themselves in Italian on the magnificent killer dog they'd acquired.

'So. He took your dog, then, the Eye-tie?' he said, easing himself on to a chair.

'He's going to be a guard dog,' Gonk told him disconsolately. 'On his estate in Italy.'

'That's what he told you, is it? Not what I heard he wanted him for.'

'What did you hear?' said Gonk. 'Come on, Sam, what are you talking about?'

'Not what I'm talking about, son. It's what they was talking about. They thought I couldn't understand, didn't they? 'Cos they was talking in Eye-tie. Only that was where they was wrong, isn't it? 'Cos I did understand. Two years I was in that prisoner-of-war camp. And when I did escape I could speak Eye-tie with the best of 'em.'

'But what were they saying about the *dog* – ?' Wurzel was impatient for Sam to get on with it.

'Going to be used for fighting. Not guarding,' said Sam, knowledgeably.

'Fighting?'

'Fighting what?' said Gonk.

'Other dogs,' said Sam. 'Well, still goes on in this country, doesn't it? So I reckon it does everywhere else. You get your dog. You train him up on raw meat. You work him up to a pitch where he's fighting mad. And then you pit him against other dogs. For money.'

'But that's terrible!' cried Sheila. 'It must be against the law.'

'Well, of course it is,' said Sam scornfully. 'So's lots of things. People still do 'em.'

'You don't think Rasputin knew that was what Luigi wanted him for –' said Gonk.

'No,' said Gerry. 'Even Rasputin wasn't that ruthless. 'If he had, he'd never have let him go.'

'Then what are we going to do about it?' said Gonk.

'Well, don't reckon there's much you can do now, is there,' said Sam. 'I mean, dog's gone, ain't it.'

There was just a chance that he hadn't – yet. In a flash Gonk was out of the door. The others followed him as he ran down the corridor and into the forecourt – just in time to see Luigi's hired car drive off with Rover panting in the back.

The kids knew the Italians were in England, at least until after Saturday's match, and so they set about trying to find Rover. First they tried the hotel. Luigi and Angelo were staying in the poshest hotel in Fairborough and Gonk and the Prof kept a watch on the outside. The Prof, who could turn on the respectability when it suited him, even managed to find out which room they were in and persuaded a chambermaid to open their door for him.

'Excuse me, I'm terribly sorry to bother you,' he said in his best accent. 'But I've left my key in my room.'

But when the chambermaid obligingly unlocked the door, there was no dog inside. Then he discovered, by inquiring at the desk, that no dogs were allowed in the hotel.

'You could have got into dead trouble, you know, if you'd just nicked him,' said Sheila. It made her feel nervous just to think what the Prof had been up to.

'So who cares about that?' said Gonk. 'I mean, we wouldn't really have been nicking him, would we? If Rasputin had realized what it was they wanted him for, he'd never have given them Rover in the first place.'

'Why don't we just go to Rasputin and tell him?' said Sheila, with her usual good sense.

'He won't listen to us,' said Gonk.

'Bet I know who he would listen to,' said Sheila.

★

So they went to Mac and told him the whole story: how Sam had been a prisoner-of-war in Italy, and understood Italian, and how he'd overheard Luigi and Angelo talking in Italian. Elaine stopped her typing to listen, and was horrified at what she heard.

'If that is what they want Rover for, it's terrible, Mac.'

'I agree with you. But what the hell do you think I can do about it?'

'We thought if you talked to Rasputin —' said Gonk.

Mac didn't think it would do any good. Rasputin had given the dog to Vincenti, and it belonged to the Italian now.

'I wonder how Rasputin would feel if he knew Luigi had lied to him,' said Elaine.

'You mean, you think I should tell him?'

'I'd say that was entirely up to you, love.' Elaine turned back to her typing.

Mac looked at her in exasperation. Why did she always have to get so involved with these damn kids and their problems?

'All right, all right, leave it with me,' he said. 'But I'm not promising anything, all right?'

In fact he forgot all about it. He was too busy thinking about Saturday's match.

Boxer set off for the match early, in his club colours.

'Are you going to win, then?' his father asked him.

'We'll slaughter 'em,' said Boxer.

'Keep out of trouble, hear,' called his mother from the kitchen.

'Who, me?' said Boxer, jokily.

'Football mad, that one,' said his mother, when he had gone.

'So was I, at his age,' said Mr Reed.

'And United were no better then than they are now.'

'Not the point, love. It's your team, you see. That's

what it's all about.' He hesitated. 'I'm turning down that job, Ethel,' he said.

'What?' Mrs Reed was stunned.

'I'm going to ring 'em first thing, Monday. Tell 'em.'

'But why?'

'Well – Kuwait. All that heat. At my age. Who needs it?'

In fact, it wasn't the heat at all. Mr Reed had picked up Boxer's unhappiness, even though Boxer was trying not to let him see it. It had surprised him – he'd thought the kids would both see it as an adventure – but now he'd thought about it he didn't want to drag his son away from the people and places he loved. 'Things are bound to start picking up here soon,' he told his wife, with more conviction than he felt. 'So what's the point in uprooting yourself. Going off to the other side of the world, practically. Just for a few bob. It's not worth it.'

He might have convinced Mrs Reed that these were his real reasons, but he didn't convince Jean. She knew at once what had made her dad change his mind. She came tearing into the junior clubroom at half-time in a real temper.

'Well, I hope you're happy now,' she said. Boxer didn't know what she was talking about.

'Dad's told you, hasn't he? He's not going for that job after all.'

'No. Why?'

'Why do you think?'

'Look, I said I would go, didn't I?' It was true, though he hadn't said it very gracefully.

'Oh yeah. You were dead enthusiastic. Real great.'

'What more could I have done?'

'If you don't know, Boxer, I can't tell you,' said Jean, and flounced out.

Out on the pitch, things were going badly for United. They'd put up quite a tussle against their opponents in the first half, but had ended up one–nil down. In the second half they didn't even seem to be trying. The ref blew his whistle for a corner and, as the winger took it, Athletic's best striker was there, niftily extricating the ball from a United defender and banging it into the net.

Luigi and Angelo, opulent in their fur coats, were sitting with Rasputin in the directors' box. They seemed to be taking a perverse pleasure in the hammering United was getting. As a third goal rolled past the United goalie, Rasputin put his head in his hands and groaned. Luigi leant over to him.

'My dear Rasputin – I've never been one to mince words. If you're going to give us a game, you're going to have to improve.'

'We might just surprise you,' said Rasputin, grimly.

Mac was in a filthy mood, too, by the end of the match. It was the worst possible moment that Gonk could have chosen to ask him if he'd talked to Rasputin about the dog.

'Look son, for God's sake,' said Mac sharply. 'Do you think I've got nothing else to worry about round here but your blasted dog?'

'Sorry,' said Gonk promptly, and scuttled off.

Almost immediately Mac regretted taking it out on the kid. He should have saved his anger for the players. Though, as it turned out, there was plenty left for them.

'Not one of your better days, Mr Murphy,' said Luigi to him smoothly in the boardroom when he had emerged from giving the players the dressing-down they deserved.

'We've had worse. And better,' said Mac, tersely. The Italian's charm irritated him. He decided to dispense with talking to Rasputin. 'Tell me, Mr Vincenti. It is illegal in Italy, is it? Organized dog fighting?'

Luigi stiffened, and the smile went out of his eyes. 'But of course.'

'But it still does go on, right?'

76

'I suppose it does.'

'You mean, you don't know?'

Luigi pretended to be mystified. 'I'm sorry. I am afraid I am not following this.'

Mac explained. 'I mean, I take it I am right in thinking that this is what you're going to use that dog Rasputin gave you for. Dog fighting. For money.'

'Mr Murphy, I can quite understand your mood after this afternoon's performance,' purred Luigi. 'But I hardly think it is very polite. To take it out on your guests.'

'Nothing to do with it, actually,' said Mac, bluntly. 'I'd be saying exactly the same thing if we'd won ten–nil. I just happen to think there's something very sick about pitting animals against each other. For kicks.'

Rasputin appeared then, grinning, and bearing a cup of tea for Luigi.

'I'm afraid, Rasputin, that you're going to have to excuse me,' said Luigi coolly. 'I have to go back to my hotel. My commiserations once more about your defeat today. But I'm sure that there is nothing wrong that a little judicious pruning won't put right. Preferably at the top –' He shot Mac a baleful look.

Rasputin, stranded with a spare cup of tea, was nonplussed. 'Was it something I said?' he asked Mac.

'Most likely something I said, actually,' said Mac, and proceeded to tell Rasputin what the kids had told him.

Boxer went home from the match feeling rotten. They'd lost, and there was the problem of Kuwait.

'It's 'cos of me we're not going, isn't it?' he said to his dad when he got home.

'That was a factor,' admitted Mr Reed.

'That's not fair, Dad.'

'Not fair?' Mr Reed was mystified.

'Course not. 'Cos that makes it all my fault you're not going, doesn't it?'

'I made up my own mind, Boxer.'

'Yeah, but it's still 'cos of me we're not going. And you all want to go. And that's three to one. So, all right, we go. All right?'

'I don't want to take us anywhere where you're going to be miserable,' said Mr Reed.

'I won't be miserable. So, all right – I'll miss things. But I'll get used to it. I want you to take that job, Dad. I mean it.'

Mr Reed shook his head at his son. He was perplexed. He'd just resigned himself to not going, and now he didn't know what to do.

Any further discussion they might have had was interrupted by a knock on the door. It was Gerry, asking Boxer if he could come out.

'Yeah,' said Boxer. 'I'll see you later then,' he told his dad.

The reason Gerry wanted Boxer was that Mac had told them that, although Rasputin was furious about Luigi's plans for the dog, he didn't think there was anything he could do. The dog belonged to Luigi now. And so the kids had decided, down at the club, to take matters into their own hands. They would get Rover back. They'd worked out that if the dog wasn't in the hotel, he was more than likely being kept at the airfield. So the boys all biked over there, Gerry, Gonk, Wurzel, Boxer and the Prof. Gonk was given a leg-up over the wire fence surrounding the airfield, and set off to find Vincenti's hangar. He did so – narrowly missing a security bloke on the way – and there was Rover, lying on a blanket in the corner. He perked up when he heard Gonk softly calling to him: too much, in fact. He barked and pulled at the rope that tethered him. Just as Gonk was about to steal in and get him, someone grabbed him from behind. Gonk gasped with fright. It was Angelo.

'What are you doing here?' he demanded. 'What do you want?'

'Nothing. I wasn't doing anything. I just wanted to see the dog, that was all.'

Angelo gave his arm a painful twist, and then thrust Gonk away from him.

'Go away,' he said. 'And stay away. If I find you here hanging around again, I'll get the police. Now move!'

Gonk moved. He left by the gate, and rejoined the others at the perimeter, when he thought Angelo wasn't looking. They debated whether to wait until dark to try again, but decided to come back first thing in the morning, although that was cutting things fine. Vincenti was flying back to Italy next day.

Early next morning they could see Rover as soon as they reached the perimeter of the airfield. He was outside the hangar, as was Vincenti's plane. But it wasn't as easy as it looked. There was a mechanic working on the plane.

'We'll never get him away without being spotted,' said Gonk, miserably.

'Yes, we will,' said the Prof. 'Watch.'

The kids couldn't believe the Prof's nerve. He left his bike, and sauntered in through the airfield gates.

'He's got rocks in his head,' said Wurzel. 'He has to have.'

But no. The Prof had learned a long time ago that, though his private education was a bit of a liability with his mates, when it came to dealing with grown-ups it could come in very handy.

'Excuse me,' he said to the mechanic in his politest voice. 'Mr Vincenti sent me. To exercise the dog before take-off.'

The mechanic barely looked up from what he was

doing. He nodded. The Prof untied the dog and, with iron self-control, walked quietly back to the gates and rejoined the others. Then Rover galloped beside them, barking with pleasure, as they cycled back to the club.

Luigi was on Rasputin's doorstep in a flash when he discovered what had happened, but Rasputin – who thought the kids deserved ten out of ten for enterprise – was not sympathetic. He pointed out that, although Luigi *said* he owned the dog, no papers had been exchanged and the dog was no longer in his possession. At this, Luigi lost his temper. He left, telling Rasputin the deal was off between their two clubs, and took Angelo in search of Rover.

They went to the junior clubroom, where they found Mac in the middle of telling the kids – without much conviction – that they had no business nicking Luigi's dog. When Luigi appeared, Mac's loyalty seemed suddenly to shift.

'I have come for my dog,' said Luigi, eyeing Rover.

'I thought it was Rasputin's dog,' said Mac.

'He gave it to me.'

'I've just talked to him, actually,' said Mac. 'He has no memory of ever doing that.'

'He's lying,' snarled Luigi.

'I'm just telling you what he said,' said Mac.

Luigi had had enough of these games. 'Get the dog, Angelo,' he said.

But, as Angelo stepped forward, Rover bared his teeth and snarled.

'Yeah. Get the dog, Angelo,' said Mac, enjoying this. 'Why don't you try it, Luigi?'

Luigi turned to Gonk. 'You. Put his lead on.'

This time Gonk wasn't co-operating.

'I'll be back with the police,' said Luigi.

'Funny that,' said Mac. 'Rasputin was just on about

them. He reckons if you persist in trying to get the dog back he'll report you to them himself. For dognapping.'

As Luigi and Angelo retired, defeated, the kids gave out a loud cheer.

'All right, shut up,' said Mac, worried that they would bring Luigi back in a fury. He began to lecture them half-heartedly again; they were in the wrong, they were lucky not to be facing charges. Then he gave up and grinned. 'Now for God's sake get that dog something to eat. He must be starving.'

10

Gradually the Junior Supporters' Club was gaining new members. One of these was a kid called Ginger Thompson, who was a mate of Boxer's. Ginger was redheaded and big for his age. He was quite a talent on the football pitch, and as keen to turn pro as Gonk had been reluctant. He hung about the ground week after week, hoping Mac would notice him, and too shy to speak to him. In the end it was Boxer who put his name forward.

'Shouldn't you be at school? Or have they gone on the four-day week as well?' said Mac, when Boxer appeared in his office.

'Half-term,' explained Boxer.

'You kids are never at school these days,' grumbled Mac. 'What do you want, anyway?'

'It's about Ginge.'

'Ginge? Some sort of tom-cat is he?'

'He's a member of our club.'

'Oh, I see. And what about him?'

'He plays soccer for our school team.'

'So?' said Mac. He could guess what was coming.

'Would you come along and watch him? He's dead good.'

'Good as Gonk?' asked Mac.

'Different sort of player. But he's still good. He wants to turn pro.'

'And why are you asking me?' said Mac. 'You're his manager, are you? On ten per cent?'

'He's scared of asking you himself.'

'Now why would anybody be scared of me? A quiet, retiring bloke like me.'

'He reckons you'd think he was just a bighead.'

'Is he?'

'Only in the box,' said Boxer, ruefully. Ginger had a habit of leaping high in the air and getting in the way of Boxer's high crosses. 'We reckon he could be another Trevor Francis,' he told Mac.

'I should be so lucky,' said Mac. But he jotted down Ginger's name all the same, and the time of the next school match kick-off.

'You're coming, then?' Boxer was delighted.

'I'll think about it,' said Mac.

Boxer knew that meant yes. He dashed out, jubilant.

'Trevor Francis,' said Mac balefully at his departing back.

The day Mac was supposed to come and watch him, Ginger didn't dare look over at the touchline, where Jenny and Wurzel and some of the others were messing about and occasionally cheering. He was scared he would see Mac there, and that it would put him off. Or that he wouldn't . . .

It was a frustrating match. Ginger himself was playing superbly, but everyone else seemed to be off form, and he felt he wasn't getting an opportunity to show what he could do. First Boxer sent him a pass which was miles too long: the goalie scooped it up before he could get anywhere near it. Then the centre-half aimed short and sent the ball to their opponents' right-back. Ginger hadn't a hope of getting it off him.

Mac arrived about twenty minutes into the game.

'Ginger's playing a blinder,' Gerry told him.

'Where's Gonk?' said Mac, surveying the pitch.

But Gonk, perhaps tactfully, had stayed away.

'Pulled a muscle,' Gerry explained.

Then their attention was caught by the game. Boxer was coasting the ball up the field. As the half-back closed in on him, Wurzel shouted.

'Cross it, Box,' and Boxer did so, kicking a good high cross towards the centre of the pitch. Half a dozen players leapt for the ball, but Ginger rose above them all, and with breathtaking assurance headed the ball accurately into the net. The kids went wild, and even Mac had to admit the kid was worth watching. He didn't take his eyes off him for the rest of the match.

He talked to Rasputin about him the following Monday.

'He's raw as an onion. Raw-boned. Clumsy,' he told him.

'Any other good points?' Rasputin was sarcastic.

'Brave as a lion,' said Mac. 'Strong. Especially in the air. A real good prospect, in fact.'

'So what are we waiting for? Let's get him signed before Birmingham or Nottingham Forest beat us to it,' said Rasputin.

Mac nodded. It was what he wanted to do, but he was a scrupulous manager. He wanted to make sure the kid knew what was involved before he spoke to his parents about him.

'So. You want to be a professional footballer, then?' he said as the boy sat, nervously twisting his big bony hands, in his office that evening after school. 'Think you're good enough?'

'Dunno,' said Ginger, blushing. He didn't want to seem bigheaded.

'You need to know,' Mac told him. 'If you're going to stand even a chance of making it. And why do you want to become a professional footballer? Because you fancy yourself with a big, flash car? The idol of the dolly birds?'

'I'd not really thought about that,' said Ginger. He was sure Mac would think those *weren't* good reasons.

'You should think about it,' said Mac. 'Because it could happen. Then again, the odds against it happening are pretty astronomical. Even if you can play a bit. Do you know how many kids sign schoolboy forms every year?'

Ginger shook his head.

'Hundreds. And do you know how many of them go on to make the grade – even in the lower divisions?'

Ginger shook his head again.

'Not a lot. The fact of the matter is there are too many professional footballers. More than the game needs. Soccer's in trouble – and clubs right across the country are cutting down their playing staffs. Because they just can't afford 'em.'

'I'd still like to have a go, Mac,' said Ginger.

'Why?'

'Well – I'm not much good at anything else,' said Ginger, frankly. 'See – I'm not very clever, really. In fact, a bit thick, me mates reckon.'

Mac grinned. 'And what about your mam and dad?'

'I've not really talked to them about it,' said Ginger.

'Then talk to them. And then, if they've no objections, get your dad to come round and see me. I'll be around most of the morning tomorrow, right?'

'Right,' said Ginger, jumping awkwardly to his feet. He couldn't wait to tell someone. 'Thanks, Mac.'

'Don't thank me, son,' said Mac. 'I'm doing what I'm doing in my own selfish interests as manager of this club. If you make it, we're the winners, just as much as you are. If you don't, you'll be the only loser.'

Ginger nodded. He reached clumsily for the door.

'Oh, and one other thing,' said Mac.

Ginger paused.

'That was a good goal today. Pure Trevor Francis,' said Mac. 'Whoever he is.'

He saw the boy's father the next day. For all Mac had been so scrupulous, Mr Thompson seemed rather aggressive and hard-done-by.

'Look, Mr Thompson,' said Mac. 'If you're here to tell me that you're against the boy signing schoolboy forms, that's the end of the matter. Nobody's doing any arm-twisting. He's a good prospect for his age, and that's all.'

But it was not the idea of his son becoming a professional footballer that worried Mr Thompson.

'The only question so far as I'm concerned is whether United's the sort of club he should be signing up with,' he told Mac.

Mac raised his eyebrows. 'Oh, I see,' he said. 'Well, it goes without saying that if you've Brian Clough and Peter Taylor knocking on your door, you'd be a mug to come to me. Have you?'

'Not so far, no,' said Mr Thompson. 'But I've every confidence they might well be, before he's very much older. If only he'd got the sense to see that, and wait.'

'So – where does that leave us, Mr Thompson?' said Mac. Personally he thought the man was rating Ginger's abilities a bit high. 'Do you want him to come to us, or don't you?'

'Frankly, I don't, no,' said Ginger's father. 'But he's adamant he's not going to sign for anybody else. So let's hear what your terms are, right?'

And so Ginger signed schoolboy forms, and started training with the other young players every evening, and at weekends. Although he was the youngest – he had only just turned fourteen – he could hold his own quite well. He worked hard, and privately Mac thought him a better player than many of the sixteen-year-olds.

It was Rasputin who persuaded Mac – against his better judgement – to give Ginger a try in the Under-Seventeens team. He wanted to see him play, and not in a school match.

'You don't find out much watching a schoolboy eleven,' he said. 'You said yourself, he's got bags of guts.'

'Which I don't want kicking out of him by putting him in too young.'

'Look, Mac – I've put money down on that kid. I like to see what I've got for my money.'

'Yes, well,' said Mac, sourly. 'I won't tell the FA if you don't.'

'Look, put him in. If it looks like it's too much for him, you can pull him off again –'

'I'll think about it,' said Mac.

A couple of weeks later, an opportunity came. Two of the Under-Seventeens team were down with flu, and Mac decided to give Ginger a try. His father didn't object, and Ginger himself was thrilled. He didn't take a lot of notice when Mac warned him not to try any clever stuff, to remember he was the youngest on the field. 'I may pull you off at half-time,' Mac said.

As it turned out, Ginger didn't make it to half-time. He was carried off the pitch to an ambulance twenty minutes into the first half. He'd done his usual trick of leaping for the ball when United took their first corner; only this time he was among bigger, burlier players, and he collided in mid-air with the opponents' goalie and fell heavily to the ground, unconscious.

At the hospital the news was bad. It was his back and it was probably broken. Ginger might be paralysed for life.

Mac was furious with himself.

'It was an accident, love,' Elaine tried to comfort him.

'I should never have allowed myself to be talked into playing him,' said Mac.

'It could have happened just as easily in a schoolboy game.'

'The fact is it didn't, though, did it? Stupid,' he said angrily to himself.

'Look Mac, these things happen, right?' said Rasputin, who had seen it happen from the directors' box. He was wearing a new fur coat, not unlike the one Vincenti had worn. Mac glanced at him with irritation.

'So, all right, it was my idea,' said Rasputin.

'Nobody's blaming you,' snapped Mac. 'I'm the manager. So far as I'm concerned, the buck stops here.'

'An *accident*,' said Rasputin.

'That could have been avoided,' said Mac, harshly.

Mr Thompson, when he arrived, felt the same way.

'Most of the boys who played against my son were at least two years older, right? Some nearly three?'

Mac nodded.

'Bobby turned fourteen just three weeks ago.'

'I know that.'

'Well, I want you to know, Murphy, that if my son ends up in a wheelchair for the rest of his life, I'll hold you personally responsible. And if there's any way I can sue – any way at all – believe me, I'll do it.'

He sat apart from the other two men, hostile and silent, as they all three waited at the hospital for the result of the emergency operation on Ginger's back. As soon as the surgeon came out of the operating theatre, Mr Thompson was on his feet, asking for news.

'He's been very lucky, Mr Thompson,' the surgeon told him. 'Very lucky. Fortunately the spinal cord wasn't cut, merely compressed.'

'Does that mean he's going to be all right?'

'Provided no further complications arise, I see no reason why he shouldn't make a complete and rapid recovery.'

Mr Thompson was not the only one to feel relief flood through him at those words; however, he was still not ready to speak to Mac and Rasputin. Not until a few days later did he come down to Mac's office.

'About what I said the other day. About the accident. I was a bit upset.'

'We all were,' said Mac. 'And I can understand just how you felt. And if you still feel like that, then of course it goes without saying that we won't try and hold on to the lad.'

Mr Thompson grinned, ruefully. 'Once he's on his feet again, try to keep him away,' he said.

It was true. Despite all he'd been through, Ginger was keener than ever. Mac reckoned he'd backed a winner.

Another kid who started coming to the club about this time was Ali Patel. Wurzel had met him one day when he was out fishing. He'd been by the river all day, with not a single bite, when this kid happened along on his smart, shiny bicycle. He'd stood and watched Wurzel for a while, and then the two boys started talking. To Wurzel he just seemed like a sprucely dressed little Asian boy, a bit younger than himself. Anyone else might have noticed that Ali's collar was distinctly grubby.

Soon after Ali's arrival, Wurzel landed his first catch. Ali was very impressed. He tagged after Wurzel back to the club, where Wurzel showed him his mur-i-al.

'Can anybody join this club?' he asked Wurzel.

Wurzel explained about the entrance fee.

'That would be no problem,' said Ali, airily. 'My father would give me the money.'

'Lucky you,' said Wurzel. They had a game of table tennis, and then Ali asked him if he could go fishing the next time he went.

'Course,' said Wurzel. 'You ever done any?' When Ali said he hadn't, he offered to lend him one of his dad's rods.

'I'd like that,' said Ali. 'That's most kind of you. When can we go? Tomorrow?'

But Wurzel couldn't make it next day, so they settled for the following Sunday.

Ali seemed a bit bothered about this. 'That fish you caught today,' he said. 'Would you sell it to me?'

'Sell it to you?' Wurzel was surprised.

'Yes.'

'I'll give it to you,' said Wurzel.

'No, no, I will pay you –' said Ali.

'Give over, will you?' said Wurzel. 'Here. Take it.'

One thing that Ali made clear from the start was that he was not short of money. He had a fantastic bike – 'a present from my father', he told Wurzel, as Wurzel laboured up the hill behind him on the model he had made himself from bits of other bikes – and he disappeared up the drive of one of the grandest houses on Hill Drive, explaining to Wurzel that this was where he lived.

Wurzel was glad he had shown him the house, when he discovered, on his return home, that he couldn't go fishing on Sunday after all. He'd forgotten that he and his parents were supposed to be going to London for the day. He rode over to Ali's house first thing on Sunday morning to tell him.

The man who answered the door wasn't very pleased to see him.

'Sorry,' said Wurzel. 'Only I had to let Ali know I couldn't make it.'

'Ali? Ali who?'

'Ali Patel,' said Wurzel. 'He lives here.'

The man cocked his head at Wurzel. 'Now, listen to me, you,' he said. 'If this is your idea of a practical joke, I don't happen to think it's very funny. You've got exactly ten seconds to get out of my garden or I'll set the dog on you.'

'But –' objected Wurzel.

'Ten seconds,' said the man. 'Now go away.'

Wurzel left, mystified. All day while he was in London – not enjoying himself very much, because it rained, and they wound up seeing a movie they could have seen at home – he pondered the mystery. That night he found Ali at the club.

'Sorry about this morning,' he told him. 'I forgot I had to go to London for the day.'

'Oh, I see,' said Ali.

'I tried to let you know, but I couldn't,' said Wurzel. He was watching Ali's face, which had gone suddenly wary. 'I came round to your house. At least I thought it was your house. But the bloke reckoned he'd never heard of you.'

'Perhaps you went to the wrong house,' suggested Ali.

'No, it was the right house all right. Number seventy-five.'

Ali stared at him for a moment. He seemed to be thinking. Then he chuckled.

'Oh I see. Seventy-five. That explains it – I don't live at seventy-five.'

'But I saw you go in there the other day,' Wurzel protested.

'No, you don't understand. Our house is behind their house. So what I do is cut through the garden.'

'Oh, I see,' said Wurzel.

Ali chuckled again. 'You thought I lived in *that* house. Oh no. Our house is much bigger than that. *Much* bigger.'

'Must be like Wembley, then,' said Wurzel. 'What's your old feller, then? Some sort of tycoon?'

'He owns a lot of shops. All over the Midlands,' said Ali. 'Come on, I'll play you at darts.'

He moved over towards the darts board.

'Oh, by the way,' said Wurzel, following him. 'You haven't forgotten you still haven't paid your entrance fee? And your first week's subs –'

'I'll pay now,' said Ali, promptly, reaching into his back pocket. 'Who do I pay?'

'Boxer,' said Wurzel.

'Funny,' said Ali. 'I had a five pound note in my pocket. I must have lost it.'

'You lost a fiver?'

'Oh well, no matter,' said Ali airily. 'I'll get some more from my father when I get home.' He raised his first dart. 'Nearest the bull for off, right?'

'Right,' said Wurzel. He couldn't understand why Ali wasn't more concerned about the lost fiver. It seemed to him there was something very odd about this Asian boy.

A few days later Ali seemed desperate to go fishing, and Wurzel bunked off school to go with him. Of course, he couldn't ask his dad for a loan of his rods on a school day, so in the end he took them without asking. The two boys went down to a quiet bit of the river, where Wurzel thought they wouldn't be seen, and Wurzel taught Ali how to cast. In the leisurely half-hour that followed, he asked Ali about his background. Had he been born over here?

'Oh no. Back in Pakistan.'

'Pretty different from here, eh?' said Wurzel.

'Oh yes. But of course, I don't remember. I was only a baby when my parents bring me back with them over here. But when they were back there – pretty damned bad scene. The whole family starving.'

'At least nobody starves over here,' said Wurzel.

'You don't know how lucky you are,' said Ali.

They fell silent then as they concentrated on their fishing. The sun had come out, and it was quiet and peaceful sitting there, until a man – who had spotted them from a copse on the other side of the river – broke the silence with an exasperated yell.

'Hoy! What do you think you're doing? These are private waters!'

'We didn't know,' began Wurzel, but the man was running along the bank towards the bridge, quite red with anger. 'Move,' said Wurzel urgently to Ali.

'What?'

'On your bike – we're poaching,' said Wurzel. He gathered up his rod, and the nets and umbrella he'd brought with him, and, his rod still assembled, and the line tangling in his spokes, he rode off on his bike, Ali following. Only when they'd put a safe distance between themselves and the gamekeeper did they stop for a breath. It was then that Wurzel discovered that Ali had left his father's rod on the river bank.

There was no choice but to go back and find it. The two boys crept to the spot where they had been fishing. There was no sign of the gamekeeper or the rod, though the flattened grass and Wurzel's lunch packet of sandwiches told them they were in the right place. Suddenly, from the other side of the river, came the gamekeeper's voice.

'Is this what you're looking for?' He was holding Wurzel's father's rod.

'Please can we have it back, mister?' said Wurzel, hopefully.

'You were poaching my private water.'

'We didn't know. Honest. Please, mister – see, it's my dad's.'

'Then you'd better send your dad to come and collect it. McAlister's the name,' said the gamekeeper. 'You'll find me up at the house.'

With that he disappeared into the copse, leaving Wurzel at a loss to know what to do. His dad was strict. If he found out about this, Wurzel would get a lot more than a ticking-off.

'I really am very sorry, Wurzel,' said Ali. They had come back to the clubroom. With no fishing to fill the time till four o'clock, bunking off suddenly seemed a pretty boring way to spend a day.

'Yeah, well, it's a bit late for that now, innit?' said Wurzel.

Ali kept eyeing the packet of sandwiches which Wurzel

had retrieved from the river bank. 'Aren't you going to eat them?' he asked, finally.

'I'm not hungry,' said Wurzel.

'Can I have one then?'

'Have 'em all,' said Wurzel. He slung the packet over to Ali.

'Thank you,' said Ali. He had wolfed the lot in a matter of minutes.

'Don't they feed you at your house, then?' said Wurzel, surprised, but then the door opened, and Mac's appearance saved Ali from finding a reason to explain his hunger. Elaine had spotted the kids coming into the club, and she and Mac had guessed they were playing hookey.

'Well, from the miserable looks on your faces, it isn't turning out to be a barrel of laughs,' said Mac. He was vastly amused when he heard what had happened, and thought Wurzel had got exactly what he deserved. Elaine, however, when he relayed the story to her, was more sympathetic.

'What are we going to do?' she said.

'What are we going to do?' said Mac. 'I'll tell you what I'm going to do, darling. I'm going to try and sort out a team for Saturday that'll win one for a change.'

'I suppose there is one thing you *could* do –' said Elaine thoughtfully.

'Forget it,' said Mac. 'No way, hear?'

But when Elaine took an idea into her head, she usually managed to get round Mac, and later that morning his car drew up outside McAlister's house. Mr McAlister was hoeing his garden when he arrived. Mac introduced himself as Mr Glossop, Wurzel's dad, and said he'd tanned Wurzel's hide for him.

'Oh yes?' said McAlister. He seemed amused. He fetched the missing rod, now broken down into its lengths, and handed it over to Mac.

'There was one other thing,' he said, as Mac climbed into his car.

'Yes?'

'Are your team going to win on Saturday, Mr Glossop?'

Mac's normally healthy complexion deepened a couple of shades. He was well and truly caught out.

'I'll send you a couple of stand tickets. You can come and see for yourself,' he said. Then he had a better idea. He would send the kids round with the tickets. And if McAlister had any dirty jobs that needed doing, well, they had nothing better to do, after all, until four o'clock.

Ali had gone home by the time Mac got back to the club, so Wurzel was told to go and call for him on his way to McAlister's with the tickets. And that was how Wurzel discovered that Ali's palatial mansion didn't exist. He cut through the garden of Number seventy-five as Ali had told him, and saw beyond, not a house with a garden the size of Wembley, but open country and ploughed fields. Wherever Ali lived, it wasn't here.

Not keen to face McAlister on his own, Wurzel decided to go home first with the rods: it would take up a bit of time. Unfortunately for him, he walked straight into Inspector Glossop, who naturally wanted to know what he was doing home at this hour and with his fishing rods. Wurzel ended up getting his father's belt across his backside after all, *and* he had to clear out McAlister's garden shed. All in all, it was a disastrous day.

He confided what had happened to Jenny that night, and when Ali appeared at the club – having forgotten his subscription this time, he told Boxer – Wurzel didn't mention the non-existent house. Instead he waited until Ali left the club. Then he winked at Jenny and strolled out after him. Unbeknown to Ali, he followed him all the way home.

Ali's journey took him through a depressed part of town, not to a grand house, but to a derelict factory.

Wurzel hid in the shadows and watched Ali let himself in through a rickety gate and cross the yard. He gave Ali a few moments, then slipped in after him. Through a high side-window, Wurzel could see a light. He hoisted himself up to the window ledge, and peered in through the murky glass. On the floor of the room was a sleeping bag, and by the light of a candle Wurzel could make out Ali cleaning his bike. His arms giving out, Wurzel jumped down softly – but his foot glanced off an old tin can and sent it rolling away from him with a clatter. Wurzel flattened himself against the wall as Ali's alarmed face pressed itself up against the window. Then he made a noise like a cat, and Ali moved away from the window, satisfied.

Wurzel went home thoughtful that night. Something was going on with Ali, and Wurzel wasn't sure what to do. He didn't want to scare him or make matters worse for him.

Next day, Ali appeared at the club, as neat and sprightly as ever, though even Wurzel, now that he was alerted, noticed that his clothes were grubby.

'Were things OK at school today?' Ali asked him.

'Yeah, no sweat,' said Wurzel. 'You?'

'I just forged a note from my father, saying I had a cold yesterday,' said Ali, smiling.

'What father?' Wurzel wanted to ask him. Instead he said, 'Crafty old you. You're quite a little villain on the quiet, aren't you?'

'Oh yes,' said Ali, pleased. 'Listen. Do you know anybody who wants to buy a bicycle?'

'Your bike?'

'Yes. I'm selling it.'

'Why?' said Wurzel.

He might have known he wouldn't get the truth from Ali.

'My father's buying me a new one. A much better one,' said Ali.

'But the one you've got's nearly new.'

'Oh no,' said Ali, smiling. 'Definitely last year's model.'

'How much?' said Wurzel.

'Twenty pounds,' said Ali.

'Blimey,' said Wurzel. The bike was worth more than twice that.

'Are you interested?' said Ali.

Wurzel hesitated. Then he decided it was time for some straight talking.

'What are you selling it for, Ali? Food?'

'What are you talking about?' Ali still smiled. 'I don't know what you are talking about. At my house I have lots of food. Anything I want –'

'I followed you last night when you went home,' Wurzel interrupted him.

The smile left Ali's face at once. 'You had no right to do that. No right at all,' he said.

'Look, .you're my mate, aren't you?' said Wurzel. 'Perhaps I can help. Are you in some sort of trouble?'

'Of course not,' said Ali. 'And it's none of your business. Now, if you are my friend, I must ask you not to tell anyone about this. Nobody. What I'm doing, I'm doing for my own reasons, right?'

'You can still tell me about it,' said Wurzel.

'No,' said Ali. He raised his hands almost as if he was trying to fend Wurzel off. 'Definitely not.'

Wurzel didn't see Ali for almost a week after that. Then one day he turned up at Wurzel's house with his bike.

'If you still want to buy my bike, I'll sell it to you,' he said. And, as Wurzel seemed doubtful: 'It isn't stolen, if that's what you're thinking.'

Wurzel shook his head.

'Will you buy if I tell what all this is about?' Ali persisted.

'Suppose I might,' said Wurzel. 'I mean, if everything was all right.'

So Ali sat down and told him the whole story. It wasn't true, what he had earlier told Wurzel, that he had come to England with his parents. His mother was dead and his father was a sick man back in Pakistan. Ali had been sent to England to stay with an uncle. His permit had only been for six months, but Ali didn't want to return to Pakistan to be yet another mouth for his father to feed. So he had stayed on – it was two years now – until someone with a spite against his uncle had told the police. Ali was quite determined he was not returning to Pakistan. He had disappeared from his uncle's house on his bike a month ago, and since then he had been living rough.

'But how do you manage?' asked Wurzel. 'I mean, about food and stuff?' He realized suddenly why Ali had wanted fish so badly.

'When I ran away I had a few pounds. And sometimes I earn a couple by doing odd jobs. But now, I'm broke. So – I sell my bike.'

'But you can't go on like this.'

'I go on for as long as I can,' said Ali. 'I tell you –' he was passionate now – 'I never go back to Pakistan. Never. I will kill myself first. So. Do you want to buy the bike or shall I sell it to someone else?'

The arrival of Wurzel's mother, home from shopping, prevented Wurzel from having to answer then and there.

'Hello, you're a new one,' she said, glancing at Ali.

'This is Ali Patel, Mum,' said Wurzel. 'Is it all right if he stops for his tea?'

'Oh no, thank you,' Ali interrupted him. 'I must go back. My parents will be expecting me. I will leave the bike outside for you, all right? You can show your parents. Let me have it back tomorrow.'

*

course the Glossop parents, when they saw the bike, ...ught, like Wurzel, that it was too good a bargain to be true. And Inspector Glossop, being a policeman, was doubly cautious. Wurzel wasn't allowed to buy the bike until he'd checked it on the police computer.

Ali, meanwhile, was hungry, and impatient about the delay. 'I don't understand,' he said. 'Why can't your father just say yes or no?'

'Well, you know what coppers are like,' said Wurzel. 'Just naturally suspicious, aren't they?'

'Coppers?' It was the first time Wurzel had said anything about his father being a policeman. Ali was horrified. 'But why didn't you tell me?' he said.

'It doesn't matter,' said Wurzel. He thought Ali might think he'd told his father all about him. 'Look, I told you I wouldn't say anything, didn't I? I promised –'

'I've changed my mind,' said Ali, abruptly. 'I don't want to sell the bike any more.' And, before Wurzel could answer, he was off.

Ali was right, as it turned out, to be so wary. Within a day or two, Inspector Glossop was down at the ground, asking his son if he knew where Ali was. The computer, fed the details of the bike, had produced a description of a missing Pakistani boy whose permit to stay in Britain had expired.

'Do you know where he lives?' Inspector Glossop asked Wurzel.

'No.'

'Bit of a mystery man, then.'

Wurzel shrugged. He waited till his father had gone, and then slipped away from the match – it was the junior match, where Ginger hurt his back – and went in search of Ali.

He couldn't find him on that occasion. He wasn't to know that Ali had heard him coming, and that as he stood in the derelict room, surveying Ali's crumpled sleeping bag, Ali was standing, tense and motionless in the corridor beyond, waiting for him to leave.

Over tea that night, he heard his parents discussing the boy. He was still missing.

'But now that he's in the area, it's only a matter of time before somebody spots him,' said Mr Glossop.

'I wonder how he's doing for food,' said his mother. 'Things must be desperate back home in his own country if he'll go to these lengths to stay here.'

Wurzel hesitated, weighing prudence with the anger he felt about the situation. Anger won. 'Why should he be sent back? He isn't doing anybody any harm,' he said, fiercely.

'It's a complicated situation, son. With arguments on both sides. In any case – there's no certainty that he will be sent back now.'

Wurzel pricked up his ears.

'Situation's changed a bit, you see,' his father went on. 'Couple of weeks ago his father died, back in Pakistan. Apparently he'd been ill for some time. So that makes his uncle here his last surviving adult relative. And he's more than willing to bring him up. He can afford to – he's got half a dozen shops in various parts of the country.'

'So that means he won't be deported?' said Wurzel.

It wasn't quite that simple, said his father. It was a decision for the Home Office, but because there had been a lot of stuff in the paper about him going missing, there was every chance they would exercise their discretion and allow him to stay.

Wurzel could hardly wait to get out of the house when he heard all this. Without finishing his tea he was off and pedalling his old bicycle across town towards the derelict factory.

This time Ali was in his room, but only just. He was packing. He'd decided it was time to move on.

'Go away,' he said when he saw Wurzel.

'I have to talk to you,' said Wurzel.

Before he had time to explain, both boys heard a door bang. Ali stiffened, and got to his feet. He went cautiously to the door through which Wurzel had just come in, and looked down the corridor. Walking towards him was a young police constable, who had noticed Wurzel's strange bike outside the factory and come in to investigate.

'You led him here!' Ali exclaimed. 'You betrayed me!' He let the door swing back and ran across the room to another door on the other side.

'No, wait,' shouted Wurzel, following him through it. He wanted to explain what his father had told him. 'Wait, you nit!' he called.

He chased Ali through echoing, empty corridors and cobwebby halls, where once machines had clattered, up stone stairs and along more corridors. Behind them thundered the policeman, heavier on his feet than either of the boys. It was Wurzel he caught.

'I haven't done anything,' yelled Wurzel, as he went crashing to the floor beneath the policeman's weight.

'Then why are you running away?' The young constable was breathless.

'I wasn't,' gasped Wurzel. 'He was. I was trying to stop him.'

Just then there was a sharp, splitting crack, and almost simultaneously a scream from Ali. The policeman jumped to his feet and ran towards an open door at the end of the corridor.

They were at a fire door, two storeys up. Ali had been making his way down the metal fire escape outside, when the top part of it had suddenly collapsed and come adrift from the wall. Ali was petrified with fear. He was stranded some way down, unable to climb back up, and frightened to go on down in case the lower part should disintegrate beneath his weight.

'Hang on,' called the constable. As he spoke there was another ominous creak. 'Don't move,' he ordered Ali. Carefully he lowered himself on to one of the remaining steps of the fire escape, his hand clutching the ledge on which Wurzel was perched. He leaned down.

'Grab my arm,' he told Ali. 'Both hands.'

And, with Wurzel grabbing his other arm to steady him, he hauled Ali up to where he was, and then shoved him on higher to where Wurzel was sitting. Seconds later, as all three of them sat safe in the doorway, there was a gathering roar, and the whole of the rest of the fire escape collapsed into itself.

'How long had you known he was hiding out at the factory?' Inspector Glossop asked his son when he heard the story.

'A few days.'

'Why didn't you tell me? Instead of going off and trying to sort out the whole thing on your own. Don't you trust me?'

'Course, Dad. It's just – well, when he told me the story, he made me promise I wouldn't tell anybody. I mean – if you break promises, you're nothing, are you?'

His father accepted that and Wurzel didn't get into trouble. In fact, he got an unexpected reward. Ali appeared at the club a few days later with a cheerful and wealthy-looking Pakistani whom he introduced as his Uncle Mukhtar. He still hadn't heard whether he could stay or not, but he was hopeful, and in the meantime he was going back to Reading to live with Uncle Mukhtar.

'Meanwhile there is one other small matter to be settled,' said Uncle Mukhtar. 'I understand that my nephew offered to sell you his bike for twenty pounds.'

'Oh yeah, but I mean, that was for food, wasn't it?' said Wurzel. 'He doesn't need to now, does he?'

'Quite so. And I have to tell you that Ali has no intention of selling it to you now,' said Uncle Mukhtar.

'Don't blame him,' said Wurzel.

'Because he is going to give it to you,' said Uncle Mukhtar.

'Give it to me?' said Wurzel, flabbergasted. 'Oh no, I couldn't. No way.'

'Oh yes, please, you must,' said Uncle Mukhtar. 'You see he will have no need of it any more because I am buying him a new one.'

'An even better one,' said Ali proudly. Wurzel glanced at him sceptically, but this time it was true.

'See – the shops I own are all bicycle shops,' said Uncle Mukhtar.

Wurzel accepted the bike after that, although he felt a bit embarrassed about it.

'What are you going to do with your old banger, then, Wurzel?' said Gonk. 'Send it to the British Museum?'

'British *Science* Museum,' said Wurzel, stoutly.

'Natural History Museum, more like,' said Jenny. And everybody laughed.

Dunmore United were looking up. They had won their last two matches, not least because Mac, familiar now with his players' strengths and weaknesses, was working on their team strategy. Some of the younger players were very good. Mac thought it wouldn't be long before some better club came after Harry Gibbons.

The gates were better too, and Rasputin was pleased. He was full of innovations. He'd decided to make the ground available to local schools for a seven-a-side competition; they played this as a curtain-raiser to United's home matches. The crowd enjoyed it, and so did the kids.

Gerry, Boxer and Gonk were all in the Whitfield Comprehensive team, and doing well. Elaine always cheered them on loudly from the stand.

'Find Gonk, Boxer,' she would shout. 'Oh, well played, Gonk. Great goal.'

'You do realize that as host club for this competition we're supposed to be strictly impartial,' Mac told her.

'You may have to as manager. I don't as general dogsbody,' said Elaine, and went on cheering as the kids won their way through to the semi-final.

Though Mac approved of some of Rasputin's ideas, he was not prepared for his next move. One Saturday, after a match, he went up to his office and picked up the local evening paper to find 'Rasputin Picks Up a Star' as the headline on the back page. Mac read on and discovered that Jock Ferguson, the well-known Scottish footballer, who had once played for Liverpool, was to join his squad.

'You never said anything about this,' said Elaine over his shoulder.

'Because I didn't know anything about it. In fact, the first I heard about it was just now in the tunnel, when one of the press boys buttonholed me for a quote.'

'Is Rasputin back from London yet?' Elaine could tell from her husband's face that he was absolutely furious.

'I don't know,' said Mac, grimly. He went off to find out.

If Mac was angry, everyone else was delighted. Cassidy thought it was a real coup for United, and Boxer Reed couldn't believe it was true. Ferguson had been his idol since he was seven or eight years old. He had pictures of him stuck up all over his bedroom: Fergie playing for Scotland, Fergie in the European Cup, Fergie in the Cupwinners' Cup.

'Well, bet you never thought you'd see the day when your idol would be turning out in a United shirt,' said his dad at home that night. Then, teasingly: 'Not a bad player in his day. Hardly Kenny Dalglish, though.'

'Dalglish! Dalglish would never have got into the Scottish side against Ferguson,' said Boxer.

'Bit of an old feller now, though. You have to admit that.'

'Not all that old,' said Boxer, loyally. 'I saw some film of him playing in America on telly last year. He was still deadly in the box –' He hesitated, suddenly struck by a thought: 'Suppose I will see him? I mean, before we leave. For Kuwait.'

'Course you will. Going to be weeks yet,' said his father.

But the memory that they were leaving had spoilt Boxer's excitement. Just as the greatest footballer of the century was coming to play for United, Boxer wasn't going to be there to see him.

Rasputin was perched on his desk, reading reports of his coup in the *Sunday Express*, when Mac Murphy strode into his office next morning.

'Morning,' he said, glancing up. 'Useful two points you picked up yesterday.' He was referring to the league match.

Mac wasn't going in for small talk that day. 'What's the idea?' he demanded.

'How do you mean?'

'Signing a player without so much as consulting me. I didn't even know you were interested in Ferguson.'

'Neither did I,' said Rasputin. He explained that he'd met him by chance in a night club, not even knowing he was back from America, and signed him up on the spur of the moment.

'Yeah, well it would be a night club where you'd be most likely to meet Ferguson,' said Mac. His objection to Ferguson wasn't simply because Rasputin hadn't consulted him; Ferguson was a big drinker who was always getting himself into scrapes which excited the newspapers but which damaged his performance on the field.

'Not any more,' Rasputin assured him. 'He's a reformed character. Got himself a nice little wife and settled down.'

Mac was sceptical. 'Why would a player like Ferguson want to come to a club like United?' he said. 'And what makes you think he'll even fit in with our set-up? The team is just beginning to hit a real rhythm.'

'Come on now, Mac. This isn't Joe Soap we're on about. It's Jock Ferguson. World-class striker. And he's in great shape. More to the point, he's box office. He'll put two thousand on every gate he plays in front of. As far as I'm concerned, he's good news in anybody's language. And if you don't like that, I'm sorry, but you're going to have to live with it.'

And that was that. No wonder, when Gerry waylaid Mac to complain that old Sam had just thrown them off the pitch, Mac was short with him.

'I'm not surprised. I'd have thrown you off myself. What's the idea?'

The kids explained that they wanted experience of the pitch before the following week's seven-a-side semi-final. Mac tore into them: it would give them an unfair advantage over the other teams; if he saw any of them near it, they'd be disqualified from the competition.

'What the hell's wrong with him today?' said Gonk, when he had gone.

'I can guess,' said Gerry. He'd overheard some of Mac and Rasputin's argument.

'He should be chuffed he's got Fergie,' said Boxer.

'That depends though, doesn't it? On what he's like when he gets here?' said Gerry, cannily.

The girls were the first people at United to meet Jock Ferguson. They were struggling with the decrepit photostat machine in Mac's office when he came in, looking for Mac.

'I'm Jock Ferguson,' he told them, flashing them one of his charming smiles.

'We know,' said Jenny weakly. She thought she had never seen such a good-looking bloke.

'Is Mr Murphy around, do you know?'

'I'll go and get him,' said Jenny, hurrying out.

While Jenny was fetching Mac, Fergie chatted up Sheila. He was very attractive to women and he knew it. He asked her all about herself, and found she was chairperson of the Junior Supporters' Club.

'Oh, I see, I'd better keep on the right side of you,

then,' he said. 'You can't have too many supporters.'

Then, when the machine jammed, he released it for her. Afterwards, in the clubroom, she couldn't praise him enough.

'What's he like, then?' Gerry wanted to know.

'Oh, dead good-looking. Like a film star.'

'We know what he *looks* like. But what's he like?'

'Oh, dead charming, isn't he, Jen?'

'Yeah, but can he still play football?' said Gonk.

'Course he can,' said Boxer. 'Remember that screamer he bent round the wall in the European Cup against Madrid –'

Gonk was doubtful. 'Three years since that, though, Boxer.'

Meanwhile Ferguson was having his first interview with Mac. Mac was civil, if a little reserved. Ferguson was positively deferential. He even made a point of telling Mac that he'd had no idea Rasputin hadn't consulted him.

'If I had, I'd have refused to sign anything until we'd talked too. Because I don't happen to think that's the way you should run a football club. Far as I'm concerned, whether I agreed with him privately or not, the boss is God with me.'

It was a slightly different tack he tried with Rasputin when he saw him later. He told him his wife was arriving on Saturday, in time for the game.

'I'll be in the team Saturday, will I?'

'As far as I'm concerned, the sooner the better,' said Rasputin.

'But is that how Big Mac feels?'

'I'll talk to him about it, all right?' Rasputin winked at Fergie, and Fergie gave him the thumbs up.

'So what's the team for Saturday, then?' Rasputin was sprawled in a chair across the desk from Mac.

'I haven't finalized it yet,' said Mac. 'I'm waiting for

a fitness check on Harry Gibbons. He took a bad knock on the shin last Saturday.'

'And where were you thinking of playing our new boy?' said Rasputin, ever so casually. 'Up front or in the middle four?'

'I haven't decided I am playing him yet,' said Mac gruffly. Elaine pretended to be very busy sorting out her papers. 'He's only trained with us twice so far, and anyway it's not just him I have to think about. It's the team as a whole.'

'You aren't seriously suggesting that a player of Fergie's ability wouldn't slot in?' said Rasputin.

'I'm talking about the team's morale,' said Mac. 'Both of our two front runners have been playing out of their skins these last few weeks. Young Gibbons especially. What are the rest of the team going to think if I suddenly drop one of them just to make room for Ferguson?'

'What are the fans going to think? When they hear the boy they all want to see can't even get into the team?'

'My decision, right?' said Mac. 'Final team selection. That was our agreed arrangement.'

'Right,' said Rasputin. But this was one battle he didn't intend to lose. 'Only when you're making your selection, just remember this. It cost me plenty getting Ferguson here. And I'm not about to pay out that kind of bread for somebody to just sit in the stands every Saturday.' And with that he slammed out.

Mac said nothing. He looked over at Elaine who was still pretending to be very busy. 'I suppose you think I'm being bloody-minded, just for the sake of it?' Mac said, quietly, at last.

'You're the boss, Boss,' said Elaine. 'Which I suppose is the point you've just made.'

Mac had made his stand. All the same he was greatly relieved when, on Friday, Harry Gibbons was still limping badly, and he could put Ferguson up front in the team without losing face. Meanwhile, all the kids were mobbing Fergie. The girls were after him for photographs to sell at the match on Saturday, and the boys gathered round him at every opportunity.

'Are you playing on Saturday, Fergie?'

'Are you going to live round here, Fergie?'

'Will you autograph this programme for me please, Fergie?'

Fergie was patient and friendly with them all. You would never have guessed he had such a low opinion of the club.

His low opinion showed itself, just a little, at the match on Saturday. He seemed bored and at times exasperated by United's patchy play. He strolled about the pitch, waiting for the others to set something up for him. But then suddenly he swung into action, and it was easy to see why he had been a world-class player. One of the United midfield players let an opponent walk away with the ball. Ferguson nipped in and winkled the ball from between his legs. Then he streaked up the pitch with it. The kids went wild.

'Come on Fergie! Come on Fergie!' Boxer was jumping up and down with excitement, as Fergie swerved past first one defender and then another, and then, spinning on a sixpence, crashed a shot high into the top corner of the net. It was the only goal of the match and it assured United of victory.

'Well, was I right or wasn't I?' said Rasputin, triumphantly.

'He took his chance well,' conceded Mac.

'Class, right? Class?'

'That was never in question.'

'You just don't like him, do you, Mac?' said Elaine, when Rasputin had gone.

'He's certainly given me no reason to dislike him. Worked hard at his training. Never questioned a thing I've asked him to do.'

'It isn't like you to take such an instant dislike.'

'I know,' said Mac, thoughtfully. 'That's what bothers me.'

The truth was, there was something insincere about Jock Ferguson which Mac didn't trust.

'Fantastic goal, Fergie,' said Boxer, admiringly, after the match, as Fergie came out to his car with his wife, a very dishy blonde in a fur coat.

'Thanks, kid,' said Fergie. 'From what I heard you put a pretty good one away yourself, today.' The fact that Fergie knew Boxer had scored in the semi-final of the seven-a-side made Boxer's day. 'So, you lot are in the final of the Sevens next home match?'

Boxer nodded.

'I'll get stripped early,' promised Fergie. 'Come and watch you. See if I can pick up a few tips.'

'Would you?' said Boxer, delighted.

'Why not?'

'Great,' he rushed off, bubbling, to tell the others.

'My hero,' said Fergie's wife, drily.

Fergie put his arm round her. 'Don't knock it, darling. It's fans like that who've helped to buy that coat you're wearing.'

Mrs Ferguson gave a little snort of a laugh. 'I still can't believe it,' she said.

'What?'

'That you've actually signed for this crummy club.'

'Experience, darling. That's the name of the game. And where would I get better experience of management than at a crummy club like this? Somewhere where you can make all your mistakes and nobody ever hears about them.'

'Aren't you forgetting? They've already got a manager.'

'Aye, so they have.' Fergie grinned. 'But it's a precarious profession, football management, love. You'd be amazed how often they get sacked.'

Jock Ferguson couldn't keep up his act of being the nice guy forever, and it was on the day of the semi-final of the Midlands Cup that he began to show his true colours.

It was an away match against Fairborough Rovers. The kids had thought they weren't going to be able to go at first, as British Rail had cancelled all their soccer specials.

''Cos last Saturday some yobboes smashed up one of the trains,' Gerry explained to Elaine. 'And mugged the guard. So we all have to suffer.'

'So, go by regular service, then,' said Elaine.

'Too expensive,' said Gonk, gloomily.

'Well – coach, then. There are bound to be coaches going.'

'We've tried for them,' said Boxer. 'Because of this train business, there isn't a seat left. Best chance we've had in years, too, of having a run in the Cup,' he added. 'With Fergie leading the attack.'

In the end Elaine, with her soft spot for the Junior Supporters, packed them all into Mac's car and drove them to the match. They sang all the way. Mac was travelling in the coach with the team – or most of them. Ferguson wasn't there. He sent a message to Mac telling him that he was going in his own car. Coaches made him feel sick and, anyway, he didn't like arriving at away games too early. He stopped at a pub on the way, for the first time in a long while.

'You aren't surely going to have a drink?' his wife was worried.

'Just a wee tonic water,' said Fergie. 'To calm my nerves. Come on.'

Ten minutes before kick-off and he still hadn't arrived at the ground. Mac was already briefing the team when he sauntered in.

'We'll have a word,' said Mac, sternly, and when he was away from the others: 'What time do you call this? In future you travel in the team coach for all away matches along with the rest of us. Understood? Now get changed, and don't ever be this late again. Or you'll be watching the game from the stands.'

Fergie gave him a murderous look as he went to get changed.

Outside, the terraces were packed. The United kids were in a big group, surrounded by a sea of Rovers colours. Their chant – 'United, United' – with the 'i' drawn out to a slow whine – was drowned by rapid bursts of 'Rovers, Rovers, Rovers, Rovers, Rovers' all around them. The two teams were evenly matched, with Fergie marked by a big, meaty bloke who tackled him promptly, but fairly, whenever he managed to get the ball. United were one-nil down as the match drew to its close. It looked very much as if they were going to be out of the Cup, when one of the midfield players put a ball through to Fergie. He streaked up the field with it, but it was clear he wasn't going to make it, as he'd done in the last match. As the full-back came in to tackle him, Fergie dived, quite deliberately, over his leg, and lay, writhing on the ground, just inside the penalty area.

The ref blew his whistle, and, as the Rovers' defenders looked at Fergie in disgust, Harry Gibbons took the penalty for United – and scored. On the terraces the kids screamed with delight, but Mac in the dug-out, and the players on the pitch, knew exactly what had happened.

'Laurence Olivier,' said the Rovers' left-half contemptuously to Fergie, who had temporarily forgotten his limp.

The whistle blew for the end of the game. Mac looked thoughtful. Ferguson had won them a replay, but at what cost to the game?

He could think of nothing to say when his opposite number, Rovers' manager, came up to him afterwards. 'That's not a football team you've got there,' he said. 'It's an amateur dramatic society. And the acting stinks.'

'So. We live to fight another day,' said Boxer's dad, when his son came home. 'Good game was it?'

'Typical cup-tie,' said Boxer.

'The bloke on the telly reckons that penalty was a bit suspect,' said Mr Reed. He'd also watched it on telly, and he agreed with the commentator. 'He reckons Fergie took a dive in the box.'

'So?' said Boxer, defensively. 'It saved the game for us, didn't it?'

'And that makes it all right, does it?' said Mr Reed.

'Everybody does it, Dad,' said Boxer. 'They'd do it to us if they got the chance.'

His dad shook his head. 'Two wrongs still don't make a right, son.'

'Look, it's the modern game, innit?'

'Win at all costs, right?'

'Right.'

'One of the reasons perhaps why I can't be bothered going to watch it any more,' said Mr Reed, and went back to reading his paper.

Boxer knew his dad was right. He was not really the hard case he tried to make out. In fact he was a fair and generous kid. It was his idea to have a whip-round to buy flowers for Elaine, to thank her for driving them all to the match and back. He went round to the Murphy's with them, alone, on Sunday morning, just as they were finishing breakfast.

'What a nice thought,' said Elaine. 'Yours, was it? Thank you, Boxer, very much. Would you like a cup of coffee?'

'No thanks,' said Boxer. 'I have to get back. Dad's got these tea-chests in. I've got to start packing my stuff.'

'How many weeks to go now?' asked Elaine.

'Couple.'

'Is Jean looking forward to it?'

'Oh, yeah,' said Boxer, disconsolately. 'Everybody is.'

'Except you, I gather,' said Elaine. Sheila had told her yesterday how unhappy Boxer was about leaving England. 'Why don't you want to go?'

'I just don't want to. I mean, I'll miss all the gang and everybody. And United for a couple of seasons. Just when Mac's beginning to put the team together.'

Elaine smiled. United was so important to Boxer, it was no good telling him they'd still be here when he got back. She said no more for the moment, but in her mind an idea was forming.

'How's the leg?' said Mac, when Fergie presented himself in his office on Monday morning.

'All right,' said Fergie.

'No after effects? From the fall?'

'I was lucky,' said Fergie.

'Not as lucky as we were,' said Mac. 'That we got a penalty out of it.'

Fergie shrugged. 'That's football, isn't it?'

'Not at my club it's not. You dived, and you know it.'

'The referee didn't think so,' Fergie grinned.

'It's not what the referee thinks that matters,' said Mac. 'It's what I think.'

'Come on, Boss,' said Fergie. 'It got us a replay.'

'We cheated our way into the replay,' said Mac. 'And if there was any way I could do anything about it, I wouldn't hesitate to do it.'

'You can't be serious,' said Fergie. 'It's happening every Saturday. All over the country.'

'I know,' said Mac, grimly. 'It's a blot on the game. Along with the so-called professional foul and all the other things some people manage to justify, just because it gets results. So don't do it again, all right? Or you're suspended.'

Fergie gave a small, mocking laugh. 'Strictly Roy of the Rovers stuff, eh, Boss? Even if some big defender is biting my legs all afternoon?'

'You get paid for it, don't you?' said Mac. He disliked the man more than ever. 'Oh, and one other thing,' he said, unwillingly. 'This seven-a-side tournament we've been running –'

'Oh aye?'

'The final's on Saturday. The chairman thinks it would be a good idea if you presented the cup to the winners before our match.'

'Right, Boss,' said Fergie. He left the office jauntily. Mac sighed. What sort of an example was Fergie to the kids?

Mac's displeasure had made no impression at all on Jock Ferguson. He wandered into the Junior Supporters' Club one evening that week with the photographs he had promised Sheila. Gonk was just telling the others about an England Schoolboy International who'd be playing against them on Saturday, but the moment Fergie came in the discussion was abandoned, and they all crowded round him.

'You didn't half put one over on that ref,' said Wurzel, grinning at him.

'I'm sure I don't know what you're suggesting, son,' said Fergie. 'That big ape of a full-back nearly chopped my legs off at the ankles.' But he winked as he spoke, and everyone laughed.

'Are these guys any good you're up against on Saturday?' he asked them.

They told him about the England International.

'Oh well. Speaking as a Scot, I reckon there's only one way to deal with an England International – and I don't have to tell you what that is. Let him know you're on the park.' He winked at them again. 'Early bath.' They all giggled. 'Don't let me down now, eh?' he said as he left. 'I've got a quid riding on you lot with one of the other players. See you.' And he was gone, leaving the girls swooning and the boys admiring.

At the seven-a-side final the following Saturday, Boxer won the toss but that seemed to be the end of the team's luck. Russell, the Schoolboy International and captain of the opposing team, was a brilliant player, who not only put a goal in the net within the first minute, but appeared from nowhere to rob Gonk of the ball, just when it looked as if he was about to equalize.

'That boy Russell's everywhere,' said Elaine, partisan as ever. 'Somebody'll have to close him down.'

Mac laughed. The kid was a pleasure to watch. 'Easier said than done, love,' he said. 'He'll be a full English International one of these days, that kid – it's written all over him.'

Jock Ferguson was not so generous towards other good players; especially when they were on the opposing side. At half-time he sauntered over to Boxer.

'That big blond kid's tearing you apart,' he said, smiling at the crowd as if he was just passing the time of day.

'We know,' said Boxer, ruefully.

'Then you know what to do about it, don't you? You can't run without legs.'

And he sauntered away again, leaving Boxer to ponder this. Perhaps this was what professional football was about. Perhaps it was just naïve to think, as his dad did, that you should play fair. After all Fergie had suggested it and he was a professional.

Mac meanwhile had seen the little interchange on the touchline; he mistrusted Fergie, and wondered what he was saying to the kid.

It wasn't long before he had a good idea. Gonk almost scored at the start of the second half, but the goalie saved it, and slung it away, a long ball, to Russell. Russell took control of it, and flew up the field, with Boxer coming in on him at a tangent. Fergie's words were hammering in Boxer's head: you can't run without legs. He'd never fouled anybody before, not deliberately, and he wasn't sure he could do it, but he wasn't going to let Fergie down and so he crashed in, a scything tackle, making sure he gave Russell a good boot across the shins as he did so. Russell gave a yell of pain as he fell, and rolled over in agony. Instinctively Boxer moved towards him to make sure he was all right, but Russell's team-mates pushed him out of the way and in a second the ref was among them.

'Off,' he said peremptorily to Boxer.

'What?' Boxer hadn't quite taken it in. He hadn't even heard the ref's whistle.

'You heard me, son. Get off.'

It was the most shaming moment of Boxer's life, as he stalked off the pitch to loud boos on all sides. He went scarlet. The crowd was a sea of hostile faces. Among them, though he couldn't see them, were Mac, looking troubled, and his father, ashamed. Russell couldn't walk. He had to be helped off the field between two players.

Beside the trophy, Fergie sat impassive through it all.

Mac was in the dressing-room almost as the final whistle blew. He took one look at Boxer's puffy, tear-swollen face, and said harshly, 'You lost. Four–nil. And just for the record, in case it was worrying you, Russell's leg isn't broken. But he'll be out for a fortnight and that'll cost him his place in the English team next week. He must love you, son.'

Boxer said nothing. He felt terrible. He didn't even stay to watch United's game, just dashed home as quickly as he could.

He wasn't at the club that night, either. The others discussed what had happened. Wurzel thought he was stupid, that he'd lost the cup for them. Gerry thought that wasn't fair, they'd been losing anyway. Gonk said what he hoped was true, that Boxer hadn't meant to go in that hard.

'So. This is where you're holding the wake, is it?' said Mac, walking in on the clubroom. He still sounded pretty grim. 'A planned tactic, was it? To clean the blonde kid out like that? Or did somebody put the idea into your thick heads? At half-time?'

The kids knew exactly what he was getting at, but nobody said anything. After a moment Mac stalked out again, disgusted with them.

At home, Boxer was wishing he could wipe the whole afternoon clean from his own and everyone else's memory.

'Whatever made you do it, Billy?' asked his father, sadly. He'd never seen this side to his son before.

'Look – it was like Fergie said, wasn't it?' said Boxer angrily. 'Somebody had to sort him out. He was murdering us.'

'Oh, *he* told you,' said his father, understanding at last.

He sighed. 'Oh well, I suppose if he told you, it was bound to be all right, wasn't it?'

'Look, just don't keep going on at me,' said Boxer, poised between rage and tears again. 'Just leave me alone, will you?'

14

Boxer wandered round in a filthy mood for days after the seven-a-side match. He quarrelled constantly with his sister, and he refused to go anywhere near the club. The other kids understood why.

'He's ashamed, in't he?' said Gerry.

'He'd never have gone for that tackle anyway – if it hadn't been for Jock Ferguson's advice,' said Gonk.

'All he said was stop him,' said Wurzel. 'Not cripple him for life.'

'We all know what he meant, man. But 'cos Boxer thinks he's so fantastic, he went in with everything.'

'There must be some way we can get him back,' said Sheila.

'What's the point?' said Wurzel. 'He'll be going abroad anyway in a couple of weeks.'

That was what gave them the idea. They would give Boxer a farewell present. And because none of them had any money, they decided on a signed, framed photograph of Fergie.

'We could get Fergie to present it to him,' said Sheila. 'He'd come down for that.'

Gonk mentioned it to Boxer at school next day. Boxer was noncommittal at first, so Gonk had another go at him during cross-country that afternoon. The two boys had stopped outside a village pub, because Boxer was crippled with a stitch.

'You will come, then?' said Gonk, as Boxer bent down, arms swinging, in an effort to relieve the pain.

'I might.'

'Everybody wants you to. Fergie's making the presentation.'

'Yeah?' said Boxer, straightening up and clutching his side.

'I think so,' said Gonk. It hadn't actually been finalized with Fergie.

'All right, then,' agreed Boxer.

'How is it now?' Gonk nodded to Boxer's stitch.

'Crucifying,' said Boxer. 'You go on. I'll see you back at school.'

That was how Boxer came to be alone by the pub wall when Jock Ferguson and his wife came out of the pub. He might not have noticed them, had they not been quarrelling loudly about who should drive. It didn't take Boxer long to see that Fergie was well plastered. It wasn't surprising, really. Fergie had had a drink problem for some time. Once he started going into pubs and having the odd drink, it wasn't long before the drink took control of him again.

Boxer did not know about Fergie's problem, of course, any more than he knew that Derek Cassidy – who did – had been in the public bar of the same pub that lunchtime and had spotted Fergie in the lounge bar through the archway behind the counter.

'You're in no condition to drive,' Helen was arguing now.

'Ah, stop havering, woman,' Fergie barked at her. He raised his arm as if he might hit her. She flinched. 'I'll drive, right,' he told her.

But something must have made him aware that he was being watched, for he turned and saw Boxer, who was wide-eyed and rather shocked.

'Hello,' he said, switching on the charm quickly. 'What are you doing out here in the wilds?'

Boxer explained that he was training for cross-country.

'Well, you don't seem to be training very hard from where I'm standing,' said Fergie. 'Want a lift? I won't tell the teacher if you don't.'

'No thanks,' said Boxer. It struck him that the teacher would be questioning his time anyway, at this rate. 'See you,' he called, and set off back to school.

'I hope he doesn't say anything. Back at the club,' said Helen anxiously. She knew what Mac would say about Fergie's drinking.

'Ah, he won't,' said Fergie, impatiently. 'Get in the car, will you?'

But the following night at the club, after he had presented Boxer with his farewell present to cheers and laughter from his mates – which made Boxer feel that at least the junior supporters didn't think he was a leper – Fergie took Boxer to one side, saying confidentially, 'Could I just have a word with you, son?'

'Course,' said Boxer.

'When you saw me yesterday. Out in the country. Well, I had had a couple of drinks, you know? See, it was our first wedding anniversary and I'd taken Helen out for a quiet meal to celebrate – understand?'

Boxer nodded.

'The thing is,' Fergie went on. 'Well, the boss might not. You ken what a stickler he is for strict training and people not taking a drink during the week. So if anybody asks – you never saw me. All right?'

'I won't say nothing, Fergie,' said Boxer, solemnly.

'Good lad,' said Fergie. He slipped a five pound note into Boxer's hand.

'I don't want anything, Fergie –' protested Boxer.

'Take it,' said Fergie. 'Go and buy yourself a ride on a

camel or something. And when you get back you can bring me a can of oil, right?'

'Right. Thanks,' said Boxer.

'See you lot again, eh?' Fergie shouted to the others. There was a chorus of good-byes.

What did he give you, Box?' Wurzel wanted to know.

'A fiver,' said Boxer. Nobody thought anything about it. To them it was just Fergie giving a generous farewell present.

'Great. Drinks all round,' said Wurzel, rubbing his hands.

Boxer shook his head. 'This is one fiver I'm never going to spend,' he said, gazing reverently at the note Fergie had handed him.

Boxer didn't tell Mac, or anybody else, about having seen Fergie drunk midweek, but Mac found out quickly enough from Derek Cassidy. His reaction was swift. When the first team list went up that week, Fergie's name wasn't on it. Fergie wanted to know why, and Mac told him. He'd been seen in the 'Golden Goose'. Despite all that Fergie said, he was out of the team for this week, and that was that. He called Boxer out of the junior club-room.

'I havena been picked for Saturday,' he told him, angrily.

'What?'

'Now, can you no guess why not?'

'No – Mac must be mad,' said Boxer.

'Oh, he's mad all right. He's furious. With me. Because of what some little bird told him about me being legless yesterday.'

'Wasn't me, Fergie,' said Boxer.

'Well, who else could it have been?'

'But it wasn't. Honest.'

'You're lying, son,' said Fergie. 'You're lying through

your teeth. You have to be.' And he stormed off to find Rasputin, to try and get him to over-rule Mac.

Rasputin couldn't see what the fuss was about.

'Look, so he had a drink –' he said to Mac.

'Not just *a* drink –'

'All right, so he had a few. It doesn't affect his performance on the park.'

'It isn't his performance on the park I'm worried about,' said Mac. 'It's the effect on the other players. The morale of the team. And if it gets around that there's one rule for them and another for Jock Ferguson, the whole thing will start to fall apart. So, as far as I'm concerned, he's dropped for Saturday, and that's that.'

'You're the boss, of course,' said Rasputin, irritated.

'That's right.' Mac wasn't climbing down this time. He knew he was right.

'At the same time there is such a thing as being too stiff-necked.'

Mac gave a small, grim laugh. 'If things start to go wrong, I'm sure you'll be the first to chop me off,' he said.

Saturday came. The team played appallingly in their replay with Rovers, and lost four-nil. By the end of the match, the crowd were screaming, 'Bring on Fergie!' while Fergie watched the debacle with considerable satisfaction from the stands. The kids were disgusted with Mac, and Rasputin had plenty to say.

'All right, just one of those days,' Mac parried.

'Yeah, well – let's just hope there aren't any more, eh?'

'Is that a threat, Mr Chairman?'

'I want Ferguson back in the team next week, right?' said Rasputin.

Meanwhile Boxer, who had been wandering round like a lost dog all week because Fergie was angry with him, hung about outside Mac's office waiting for a word.

'What do you want?' snapped Mac, at last.

'I just wanted to ask you something,' said Boxer.

'Well, ask me later,' said Mac. 'You should know better than to come bothering me right after a game.'

'I just wanted to know whether you told him or not,' Boxer persisted.

'Told who, what?' said Mac, exasperated. Then he remembered. Boxer had asked him to tell Fergie it wasn't him who grassed. 'Elaine told him,' he said.

'Thanks,' said Boxer, with relief, and went in search of Fergie.

He had a while to wait until he appeared with Helen. Boxer hung back until they were getting into the car, and then approached him timidly.

'Fergie –'

Fergie turned. He was oblivious of the fact he'd given Boxer a miserable week. 'Oh, hello,' he said.

'Didn't half miss you out there today,' said Boxer, hungry for forgiveness.

Then Fergie remembered, 'Look, I'm sorry I was a bit rough on you the other day. Only I was that wild, you know?'

'Course,' said Boxer, eagerly.

'See you around, then,' said Fergie, cheerily. Then he had an idea. 'In fact – tell you what. Are you doing anything special this Sunday afternoon?'

Boxer shook his head.

'Then how would you like to earn yourself a couple of quid? See I'm in this golf match tomorrow and I could use somebody to caddy for me.'

'What do I have to do?'

'Just lug my bag around the course for me, that's all.'

'Yeah. Great,' said Boxer. His spirits had lifted. He was back in Jock Ferguson's good books again.

His spirits lifted still further when, that evening, Elaine came into the clubroom and asked him if he'd like to lodge with her and Mac while his parents were in Kuwait. He would be able to see the club play every week ... he would be able to see Fergie. Elaine said that now she knew he was agreeable to the idea she would go and talk to his parents next day.

Fergie picked him up from the clubhouse in his red sports car at two o'clock. The golf club was quite a long way out of town. It was a nice, breezy afternoon, and Boxer enjoyed following his idol – who was almost as good at golf as he was at football – around the hilly course.

It was after Fergie had finished his game that the trouble started. He disappeared into the clubhouse, and stayed there all evening, coming out only once, early on, with a can of coke and a packet of crisps for Boxer. Darkness fell, and Boxer felt progressively colder and hungrier. He longed to go home and find out what his parents had said about Elaine's suggestion. From time to time he stood up and walked around. Through the club windows he could occasionally glimpse Fergie buying himself more drinks.

It was after ten o'clock when Fergie finally emerged from the club and, when he did so, Boxer could see at once that he was very drunk.

'Did you think I was never coming?' he said, putting an arm round the boy.

'It's just my mum. She'll be worried,' said Boxer.

'No sweat,' said Fergie. 'We'll have you home in no time.' He was slurring his words, and he lurched unsteadily towards the car. Boxer followed, worried. He could see Jock was in no condition to drive.

'You've not put your lights on, Fergie,' he said, timidly, as Fergie swung the unlit car out into the dark country lane.

'So I haven't,' said Fergie. He grinned. 'I was wondering why I couldna see very well.'

He flicked his lights on full beam, and put his foot down

hard on the accelerator. Boxer clutched his knees in fear. They were travelling much too fast, careering along the winding lane at about fifty. He stifled a cry as it seemed they must clip the stone wall by the side of the road. Then, as he saw an old man crossing the road in the light of Fergie's headlights, he thought he must slow down. He looked across at Fergie. He was lighting a cigarette, and having difficulty bringing the flame to its tip. His eyes weren't even on the road.

'Look *out*!' screamed Boxer.

At the very last moment, Fergie saw the old man. He swerved violently, almost throwing Boxer through the windscreen, and there was a sickening thump. Boxer, twisting to look behind him, saw a dark lump in the road.

'You hit him!' he cried in consternation.

'Just missed him,' said Fergie.

'You hit him. You definitely hit him.' Boxer thought maybe Fergie was too drunk to understand.

'Shut up,' said Fergie. He turned on to the main road and drove faster than ever.

15

Fergie didn't stop the car until they were on the outskirts of town. Then he pulled up by a telephone box.

'Now you listen to me, son,' he said. The accident seemed to have sobered him up, although he was trembling. 'I didna dare stop, understand? I've been done once for drinking and driving, and if they get me again that's me banned from driving for years.'

Boxer sat and stared at him in horror. He found it hard to believe Fergie was thinking only of himself, when a man was lying injured in the road not half a mile away.

'Now this is what I want you to do,' said Fergie, seemingly oblivious of Boxer's reaction. 'I want you to go to that telephone box now and dial 999. When she answers, ask for an ambulance. Tell them there's been an accident and where it is. But don't go giving them your name or address. When you've passed the message, just ring off, right?'

'Why have I got to do it?' said Boxer, sullenly.

'Because if I do it, they'll recognize the accent, won't they?'

'You should have stopped,' said Boxer.

'All right, I should have stopped,' agreed Fergie impatiently. 'The fact is I didn't, and it's too late to go back now. Now are you going to make that phone call?'

Boxer hesitated. Then he remembered the man lying like a bundle in the road. He went and made the call.

'One more favour, son,' said Fergie as he drove him home after it. 'If anyone finds out about this, it's gaol for me for sure. I mean it, Boxer. I'm relying on you.'

Boxer's mother opened the door the moment she heard the car draw up outside. She'd been worrying about him and had made his father phone the golf club to see where they were.

'We thought you must have had an accident,' she said, as Boxer came inside.

Boxer glanced at her sharply.

'Are you all right?' She knew he wasn't by his pale, exhausted face.

'Course.'

'I'll get you your tea –'

'No thanks,' said Boxer. The idea of food made him feel quite sick.

'Something's happened,' said his father. Boxer didn't even seem interested to hear that Elaine Murphy had been round to see them, or about the offer she had made.

When Fergie reached home he examined his car in the privacy of his garage. The nearside wing was dented and the headlight was broken. Fergie ran his finger over the damage and grimaced in distaste. There was blood on his finger. He shivered, then went and fetched a bucket of water, and washed it away thoroughly. Then he washed the sponge to make sure there was no blood on that.

Next morning he took the car to a garage in town, and told the mechanic he'd had an argument with a lamp-post. Could he fix it quickly? The mechanic agreed. Jock Ferguson was the sort of man most people liked to oblige.

'What the hell time do you call this?' Mac demanded, as he strode into the dressing-room and found Fergie changing into his strip at quarter to eleven.

'Sorry I'm late, Boss,' said Fergie easily. 'I had to drop my car off at the garage.'

'Then do it in your own time, not mine,' growled Mac.

'Yes sir,' said Fergie. He clicked his heels and saluted mockingly. He didn't see why he should turn up for the post mortem on a match in which he hadn't even played.

'Don't try and take the mick out of me, son,' said Mac. 'There's only one boss around here, and you're looking at him. If you want to play for me, you'd better realize that.'

Fergie was jumpy that morning, what with his hangover and anxiety about the accident. His temper snapped.

'Aye well, look, I'll tell you what, Boss. Let's cut our losses right away and say I don't want to any more. Not if I'm going to be treated as if I was still a baby. And just leave it at that, eh?'

'Your decision. Not mine,' said Mac.

'That's right,' said Fergie. 'And I've just made it.'

The story was all over the papers by evening. The kids couldn't believe it.

'Hey, have you lot seen the paper? Jock Ferguson's walked out on us –' said Gonk, dashing into the clubroom.

'What?'

'Him and Mac have had a ding-dong and he says he'll never put a United shirt on again.'

'They *can't* let him go,' said Gerry, appalled. He's the only decent player we've got. Let me see –'

They all crowded round the paper to read the lead story on the back page. All except Boxer, whose eye was caught by the headline on the front of the paper: 'Hit and Run Victim Still Serious. Mystery Caller Sought'. So the man was still alive, at least. Boxer hadn't been able to get him out of his head all day.

'His story is that you goaded him into it,' said Rasputin, when he and Mac had their inevitable confrontation about Fergie's resignation.

Mac shook his head. 'I simply made it clear who the boss was – that was all. If he isn't prepared to accept that, then he's better off leaving. As a matter of fact, I've already had Southampton on the phone about him.'

'Yeah, well you can tell them where to go for starters. He stays.'

'Look,' said Mac. 'There's no point in trying to hang on to players who want to go. They're bad news for the club and bad for the team.'

But Rasputin was adamant. Fergie was staying.

'I'll get him to apologize to you,' he told Mac.

'It's too late for that.'

'Don't make me have to choose between you, Mac.'

'Seems to me you already have,' said Mac, angrily. 'You'll have *my* resignation by the end of the week.'

The kids learned of this latest drama through Boxer. He'd talked to his parents about Elaine's offer, and went round to see Mac and Elaine and tell them that it was OK.

'Good,' said Elaine, pleased.

'Yeah – except there is a bit of a problem now,' said Mac. He explained that he'd had a barney with Rasputin, and Boxer guessed at once that it was over Fergie.

'Of course, I haven't got another club lined up yet,' Mac told him. 'But I certainly hope to have soon. And when I do – well, it's almost certain I'll be leaving the area. Which, as far as you're concerned, rather defeats the object of the exercise, doesn't it, son?'

'Suppose it does, really, yeah,' said Boxer, dispiritedly.

'Sorry about that,' said Mac.

'Yeah. Oh well – thanks anyway. I'd better go, then. See you.'

'Who'd have thought it?' said Wurzel, when he told the others. 'Us getting the great Jock Ferguson here would have caused all this trouble.'

'Yeah well, tell you what, man,' said Gonk. 'I don't suppose you'd agree, Boxer – but if I had to choose between keeping Mac and keeping Fergie I'm for Mac every time.'

'Matter of fact, Gonk,' said Boxer sombrely. 'I'd say you was dead right.'

The others looked at him startled, not quite certain they'd heard him right. Then they started talking about what they could do. Wurzel suggested they should invade the pitch at the next home match to show Rasputin how they felt.

Jenny was scornful. 'All they'd do is throw us off the ground.'

'Yeah, and then sling us out of here as well,' said Gonk. 'Then we'd have lost Mac *and* the club.'

'What about a petition?' suggested the Prof. 'We can get all the Junior Supporters organized to get signatures. Hundreds of them. All asking for Mac to get his job back. Then we take it to Rasputin and show him.'

'Still won't budge him,' said Gerry. 'Not him.'

'Worth a try though, isn't it?' said Sheila. 'Anything's worth a try.'

And because nobody could think of a better idea, they agreed on a petition.

Meanwhile Fergie, who had managed to put Sunday evening's drinking and its aftermath firmly to the back of his mind, was seizing his opportunity. He called to see Rasputin, and said how surprised he'd been by Mac's resignation.

'I think he's being pretty foolish,' he told Rasputin. 'I mean, let's face facts, he's not had much of a track record as a manager so far.'

'Oh, I dunno,' said Rasputin, who liked Mac, and didn't want to run him down like this. 'He's done all right by us.'

'He's done *all right*,' said Fergie, disparagingly. 'But he hasn't done much before that. And walking out on this job isn't going to help his career at all. I'd say he'd be pretty lucky to find himself another place, actually.'

'Mmm,' said Rasputin, not wishing to agree. 'So. Seeing he is leaving, where does that leave us?'

'I've no quarrel with you, Mr Jones. Or the club.'

'Right,' said Rasputin, relieved. 'So that's settled then. You're staying, right?'

'You've still got me under contract,' said Fergie, piously. 'And the word I got was that you won't sell me, anyway. As a matter of fact I was going to come and talk to you –'

'Oh?' Rasputin pricked up his ears.

'Well – if he is going, that means you're in the market for a new manager, right?' said Fergie, with a grin. And before he left Rasputin's office, he'd talked himself into Mac's job.

'Messed things up for you, Mac leaving, I suppose,' said Gerry sympathetically. He was round at Boxer's house, trying to cheer him up.

'Yeah,' said Boxer. And then he added morosely, 'I dunno. Perhaps I'll be glad to go. Get away from round here.'

'What makes you say that?'

'I dunno,' said Boxer, and lapsed into brooding silence.

Gerry tried again. 'What did you mean?'

'What?'

'Last night. About Mac and Fergie. And choosing between them.'

'What I said,' said Boxer. 'I mean, we owe Mac, don't we? We don't owe Fergie anything.'

'You've gone off him then, have you?'

Boxer shrugged.

'Since the golf match, right? Did you have a row, then?'

'No,' said Boxer. He sipped his cup of coffee moodily.

'Bet there was something,' Gerry persisted. 'Does help, you know, Box. To talk.'

'Can't,' said Boxer, tersely.

'Course you can. To your mates.'

Boxer hesitated. He was longing to get it off his chest to someone.

'Look – promise me. Promise me you won't tell anybody. *Nobody.*'

Gerry promised. And when he heard what Boxer had to tell him he was in no doubt that Boxer ought to go to the police.

At the club Mac learned who his successor was when he walked into his office and found Fergie sitting at his desk.

'What do you think you're doing?' he demanded.

'Waiting for the press,' said Fergie, calmly.

'The press?'

'We're having a bit of a press conference. Me and Mr Jones. To announce the name of the new manager.'

'You?' Mac couldn't believe his ears.

'That's right. Matter of fact it's been on my mind for a long time, you know? To get out of playing and into player-coaching. Preferably with some fleabitten outfit like this one where I can learn the ropes without doing myself too much damage.'

'So that's why you agreed to come here,' Mac said. Everything had suddenly fallen into place, including his own instinctive suspicion of the man. 'You were after my job all the time, weren't you?'

'Let's say it was a happy coincidence, that when a vacancy came up, I did just happen to be on the spot. And available,' said Fergie, smugly.

Mac shook his head. 'Poor United.'

'Aye well, we'll just have to see about that, eh?'

'Get out of that chair,' said Mac, advancing. 'I haven't left it yet.'

Fergie saw the anger in Big Mac's eyes. He rose promptly and came round to the front of the desk, offering a handshake.

'Look Mac, it's a hard game, football. Dog eat dog,' he said placatingly. 'So no hard feelings, eh?'

Mac ignored the outstretched hand. 'There are dogs and dogs,' he said contemptuously. 'Now get out.'

Fergie had achieved what he wanted, but he couldn't but be aware of the mounting hostility among the fans. First of all there was the petition. The Junior Supporters had collected literally thousands of signatures. Then there was the atmosphere of frank dislike he felt in the junior clubroom. Even Boxer seemed to shun him. He declined a second invitation to caddy for him.

'Sure?' Fergie asked him. 'There's a fiver in it for you. Ten if I win again.'

'No thanks,' said Boxer.

'Suit yourself. Your loss,' he began to walk away, then remembered that it wouldn't do to get on the wrong side of the kid. He stopped. 'Oh, and by the way, son – now that I'm the new gaffer around here – if you ever want any free tickets you've only got to ask, all right?'

He winked at Boxer. Boxer looked away. He could hardly bear to look at Fergie now. The image of the man lying injured in the road was with him day and night. He wished he knew what he should do. He wished Fergie could get caught without him grassing.

In the end that was what happened. Unknown to Fergie, there had been a witness of the accident, a woman who had not only described Fergie's car to the police, but managed to get down most of the number. When PC Morris came down to the club to talk to Ferguson, Fergie tried to brazen his way out of it. He insisted PC Morris speak to his passenger.

Mac was in the clubroom, saying his good-byes to the kids when Fergie came hurrying in.

'Here, this is the kid here. Boxer,' Fergie told Morris. 'Now, he'll tell you. Now listen to me, Boxer,' and he explained that he was being accused of the hit-and-run accident. 'Now you were there, son. You're my witness. You tell him we never hit anybody.'

Boxer hesitated.

'Well, Boxer?' said the policeman.

'Look, what are you waiting for?' said Fergie impatiently. 'This is important. I could be in serious trouble if you don't back me up.'

'Let him speak for himself,' said Mac. He didn't like the way Fergie was hectoring the kid.

'Tell him the truth,' said Fergie.

'That's right.' Gerry spoke up, tensely, from the back of the room. 'Tell him the truth, Boxer. Go on. Tell him the truth.'

There was a split second's silence. Then –

'We did hit somebody,' said Boxer, clearly.

'You're a liar!' shouted Fergie.

'I wanted him to stop but he wouldn't! He just wouldn't!'

'He's lying, I tell you,' said Fergie. He gestured round Mac and the kids. 'They've all got it in for me, this lot, because they blame me for taking his job away from him.'

It was no good. Fergie had to go down to the police station with PC Morris, where he was charged with dangerous driving and failing to stop after an accident.

'What on earth made you keep your mouth shut about this?' Mac demanded of Boxer.

'I didn't want to be the one who snitched on him, did I?' said Boxer.

'That isn't snitching,' said Mac, appalled. 'That's

withholding evidence. Come on, let's find your dad, and take you down to the cop shop to make your statement.'

There was no question of Ferguson coming back to the club when Rasputin heard what had happened. He went round to Mac's that same evening, and suggested, tentatively, that as he hadn't opened Mac's letter of resignation Mac might like to tear it up.

Mac looked at the proffered envelope and didn't immediately take it.

'So long as if I do take it back, it is clearly understood –' he said.

'Yeah, yeah, I know,' said Rasputin. 'You're the boss.' He tore the letter in half. 'Stubborn as a mule you are.'

'Takes one to know one,' said Mac.

The kids were delighted with his return as manager. There might be no stars in the team now, but they had Mac who was going to train them a team and make United great. And they had a clubroom, and Boxer had somewhere to stay while his parents were in Kuwait, and a clear conscience.

They celebrated it all with a disco. When Mac and Elaine arrived they were deafened by the music from the loudspeakers.

'Are we going to have to shout at each other over this all night?' bawled Mac to Jenny.

'Do you mind?' shouted Rasputin beside him. 'That just happens to be my only golden disc.'

Mac chuckled. 'No wonder you retired,' he said. He raised his can of coke. 'Cheers. To United –'

'To United,' chorused the kids.

THE PIGMAN'S LEGACY
Paul Zindel

Consumed with guilt and grief since the death of Mr Pignati, John and Lorraine determine to help another old man they find in his abandoned house. They force their way into his life, full of plans to make amends for their past mistakes, but things go very wrong and they begin to wonder if the Pigman's legacy is simply too much for them to handle.

A QUESTION FOR ORION
Rosemary Harris

Fleeing from the terror of the Freaks, who have overrun and enslaved Western Europe, Jan and her friends realize that their only hope for freedom is to fight back. An exciting but disturbing tale of a future world dominated by barbarism.

EMPTY WORLD
John Christopher

Neil Miller is alone after the death of his family in an accident. So when a virulent plague sweeps across the world, dealing death to all it touches, Neil has a double battle for survival: not just for the physical necessities of life, but with the subtle pressures of fear and loneliness.

TULKU
Peter Dickinson

Escape from massacre, journey through bandit lands,
encounters with strange Tibetan powers – and beneath
the adventures are layers of idea and insight. Winner of
both the Carnegie and Whitbread Awards for 1979.

SURVIVAL
Russell Evans

High tension adventure of a Russian political prisoner
on the run in the midst of an Arctic winter.

MISCHLING, SECOND DEGREE
Ilse Koehn

Ilse was a Mischling, a child of mixed race – a dangerous
birthright in Nazi Germany. The perils of an outsider in
the Hitler Youth and in girls' military camps make this
a vivid and fascinating true story.

A LONG WAY TO GO
Marjorie Darke

The fighting rages in France, and posters all over London
demand that young men should join up. But Luke has
other feelings – feelings that are bound to bring great
trouble on him and the family. Because nobody has
much sympathy for a conscientious objector – perhaps
the only answer is to go on the run.

THE ENNEAD
Jan Mark

A vivid and compelling story about Euterpe, the third
planet in a system of nine known as the Ennead,
where scheming and bribery are needed to survive.

THE GHOST ON THE HILL
John Gordon

An eerie story which shows the author's ability both to
portray delicate relationships and also to evoke a chilling
sense of the unknown.

THE TWELFTH DAY OF JULY
ACROSS THE BAICADES
INTO EXILE
A PROPER PLACE
HOSTAGES TO FORTUNE
Joan Lingard

A series of novels about modern Belfast which highlight
the problems of the troubles there, in the story of
Protestant Sadie and Catholic Kevin which even an
'escape' to England fails to solve.